CUL-DE-SAC

by the same author

Who Goes Next?
The Bastard
Pool of Tears
A Nest of Rats
Do Nothin' Till You Hear From Me
The Day of the Peppercorn Kill
The Jury People
Thief of Time
A Ripple of Murders
Brainwash
Duty Elsewhere
Take Murder...
The Eye of the Beholder
The Venus Fly-Trap
Dominoes
Man of Law
All on a Summer's Day
Blayde R.I.P.
An Urge for Justice
Their Evil Ways
Spiral Staircase

CUL-DE-SAC

John Wainwright

St. Martin's Press
New York

Library of Congress Cataloging in Publication Data

Wainwright, John William, 1921–
  Cul-de-sac.

  I. Title.
PR6073.A354C8   1984   823′.914   84-2109
ISBN 0-312-17847-6

First Published in Great Britain by Macmillan London Ltd.

First U.S. Edition

10 9 8 7 6 5 4 3 2 1

This one . . .
for Ralph and Eileen

PART ONE

The Diary of John Duxbury

. . . and, on the whole, not a very enjoyable day.

SUNDAY, 31ST OCTOBER

Today is my birthday. A very mixed fifty years. Some moments of pleasure. Happiness, even. But many more periods of dull misery. As for the rest . . . mediocrity is, I think, the word.

When my son comes to read these diaries of mine, which hopefully he will so do when I am gone, he might find crumbs of wisdom. Some small truths which may help him avoid the trap in which I now find myself. I must, therefore, address this diary to him. I must keep him in mind as I write. It must contain more than it has done previously. More than my own private thoughts and musings.

I must also explain the mistakes I have made. The hidden faults behind the life of a fifty-year-old man of moderate means who, on the face of it, is held in respect. Who has done nothing deliberately wrong, but at the same time nothing of outstanding importance. A moderately well-educated man. Moderately well-read. Moderately successful in business. Moderately admired by his fellows. Moderately . . .

Damn that word!

'Moderately'. Who in his right mind wants to be merely 'moderate'? In anything. In *everything*. It smacks of mediocrity. It hints at a lack of ambition. More than that, it screams to the high heaven of a lack of real effort. Better, surely, to try for blinding success and achieve only blazing failure. Even headline failure is a form of success. At least you are known. More than your immediate family and acquaintances know that you have lived. That you have *been*. Not immortality, of course, but more than a cold, nameless statistic on some census form.

To brighter thoughts . . .

9

This being both my birthday and Hallowe'en, Harry and Ben took us out to dinner. Fine food and a nice restaurant. I can't remember a more pleasant evening. She will, I am sure, make Harry a good wife. Maude, I know, has doubts; but Maude has doubts on most things and refuses to be moved. I try to understand her, but find it very difficult sometimes. Why, for example, will she insist upon calling our daughter-in-law 'Benedicta' when everybody else calls her 'Ben'? She *looks* a 'Ben'. She *acts* a 'Ben'. She much *prefers* 'Ben'. As I understand things, she was christened 'Benedicta' as a sop to her Italian grandmother, but since childhood everybody has called her 'Ben'. Only Maude uses the name 'Benedicta'. Even I can see it annoys slightly, and forms an invisible barrier between mother- and daughter-in-law.

Come to that, why must she still call Harry 'Henry'. Harry has been 'Harry' since his schooldays. Why *not* 'Harry'? It is a perfectly good name. Not really a nickname. Every Henry seems to be called 'Harry'. Every John seems to be called 'Jack'. King Henry V was called 'Hal', and if shortening names is good enough for royalty why should the family Duxbury have reservations?

(Or was it Henry VIII? Or both?)

I care not. I will continue to call them Harry and Ben (a) because they like and prefer it, and (b) because it suits their easy-going happiness. God grant that they do not lose that happiness.

At this moment Maude is in bed. She retired more than an hour ago. The usual routine. At a guess she will be surrounded by pillows, reading one more 'romantic novel'. Paperback, of course. It is a world in which she seems to live. A Never-Never-Land, where bowels and bladders are never emptied, where babies arrive without the act of copulation, where women swoon whenever male lips touch theirs. And, if I tend towards bitterness, I think I have cause to be.

I sometimes wonder how many marriages have been wrecked because of this great outpouring of super-refined trivia. How many decent, ordinary (albeit not very intelligent) women such trash has transformed into make-believe 'ladies', and how many husbands have suffered accordingly.

Enough of this petty moaning. I have had a pleasant enough day. People who matter to me have remembered my birthday and sent me cards. Harry and Ben have bought me a new pipe. Dr Plumb . . . my favourite make.

To my bed. To my lonely bed. Fifty years of life, and for the last three I have been celibate. Here in the privacy of my diary I can indulge myself. Tell you, Harry, of the foolishness of your mother. Such foolishness! We sleep in the same room, but have separate beds. Because (God help us!) your dear mother truly believes that after the age of forty-five a true gentleman – I should have written the word in quotes – a true 'gentleman' casts such thoughts from his mind. He learns to 'control himself'.

Fortunately, I am not a carnal man. Equally fortunately, I pride myself on a wry sense of humour. My son, the situation demands a sense of humour, as you will discover in good time. Humour or outrage. And outrage would be wasted on your dear mother.

TUESDAY, 2ND NOVEMBER

What a ridiculous day!

I find that, by keeping this occasional diary, I can rid myself of what would otherwise be an exasperation bordering upon outright anger. I can (with difficulty sometimes) hold my temper in check, pending this pre-bedtime recording of what, by any normal yardstick, has been an episode based upon outrageously bad manners.

I need hardly remind you that, when the spirit moves her, your dear mother has a waspish tongue. She denies it, of course. She believes (truly believes, I think) that her periodic and, these days, increasingly regular spats of ill-temper are not spats of ill-temper at all. Remind her of what she has said. Quote her, word for word. She will look shocked and hurt, then twist the words, mis-quote them and repeat them in a most reasonable tone of voice. '*That's* what I said,' she will insist. But in fact had she said 'that', and had she used the moderate tone she insists she used, nobody would have been offended and I, personally, would not have been embarrassed.

11

Harry, my son, believe me.

I love your mother dearly. I would have married no other woman. I would have no other son but you, nor would I have any woman other than my wife as that son's mother. I make that plain. No qualifications. Believe that and thereafter you may criticise as much as you wish.

Such a stupid, petty reason for an almighty (and, in the main, one-sided) quarrel. A tiny crack in a teacup. A hair-line crack.

At midday I met Maude as arranged. New curtains for the lounge. To choose them and arrange to have them fitted. It started then. 'The mood' was on her. Could we afford this? Surely we couldn't afford that? In effect she was arguing with herself. Decisions! Why, in Heaven's name can't she ever make a comparatively simple decision? She had complete freedom. Colour, style, everything. My only contribution was that they must be good quality curtains, capable of lasting for years. I suggested velvet, and was told not to be ridiculous. Thereafter, I kept my opinions to myself.

It took us five shops before a decision was reached and, even then, it was only a half-hearted decision. Even I could see that. I suggested we try again, another day. Other shops. I was held up to ridicule in front of the assistant. A mere man! What did *I* know about soft furnishings? What did *I* know about colour schemes?

I think the choice was made out of sheer petulance. I hope I'm wrong. I hope she *does* like them. I know I bit my tongue, made out the cheque and suggested a quick lunch before I returned to the office and she took a taxi home.

Damnation, it *is* a good café. A clean café. Spotlessly clean. I've used it too many times not to be sure. I know the manager. He sometimes comes to my table and chats. We have a mutual interest in amateur photography, and he's a member of the local society. He's anxious that I join but, what with making up the firm's books and filling in those infernal VAT returns in my own time at home, I haven't the time. Come to that I never *have* belonged to clubs or societies. Never. It isn't something I yearn for. It isn't something I miss. I like my home. The comfort of my home. I am perfectly satisfied with the company of Maude . . . when 'the mood' is not on her. I suppose I'm a shy man. It doesn't matter. For whatever

12

reason, I have never joined clubs and such.

Nevertheless, I know the man and respect him. He runs a good café. I suppose it can be said that I know the waitresses. Most of them. Not by name, of course, but by sight. They look upon me as a friend of the manager and are anxious to please. That, in turn, pleases me. But is that a crime? Is that something of which to be ashamed?

I ordered scrambled eggs on toast. Maude ordered chocolate cake. We both asked for tea.

My first inkling that something was wrong was when Maude snapped her fingers and beckoned for the waitress.

She snapped, 'I wish to see the manager,' and I wondered what on earth was wrong.

At a guess the waitress was still in her late teens (certainly not older than the very early twenties) and, after an initial look of stunned surprise, she said what she should not have said to a woman like Maude in those circumstances.

'What is it, luv? Can I help?'

My God! Had the poor girl used bargee language, the effect could not have been worse. Who was *she* calling 'luv'? What sort of respect did the youngsters of today have for their elders? Couldn't she understand plain English? The manager had been asked for. Did the manager hide behind the impudence of a cheap little tart?

The waitress was close to tears as she brought the manager and (naturally) the manager was both puzzled and annoyed, and asked *me* what the trouble was. I didn't know, but before I could say so, Maude took over.

A cracked cup, no less. I probably should have written no *more*. We had to look for the crack. Virtually search for it. It was only visible when the cup was held in a certain position. With the light striking it from a certain angle. Certainly it wasn't *obviously* cracked.

I think, for the first time in my life, I was genuinely ashamed of Maude. It is (you have my word for it, Harry), it is a terrible thing for a man to be truly ashamed of his wife. If he loves her, that is. Excuses are empty. They mean nothing, because they are merely words. Loyalty (I suppose it's loyalty) insists that he either back her up or remain silent. I chose to remain silent. It was Maude's

13

complaint. A trivial complaint, or so *I* thought. She'd opted to blow it up into a full-scale row, and I wanted no part of it. I left them to it. I handed the manager a fiver before I left. Enough (and more) to pay for the meal *and* a new cup. Conscience money, I suppose. I doubt if I shall use that café again. A pity. It's a very good little café, but after Maude's outburst . . .

As I handed him the note, the look the manager gave me spoke volumes. A look of pity mixed with understanding.

Damn the man! I do not want pity. I do not need 'understanding'. I want Maude, as she once was. As she was when I married her. Not younger. Not that. Age has nothing to do with it. I want her happy. Less antagonistic. Prepared to accept life as it is, knowing that nothing and nobody is perfect. I want her to have joy from life. To have joy and, in having joy, to give joy. Not to fight and scratch her way through life, as she does.

Perhaps I'm a fool, asking the impossible. Sometimes it seems so.

This evening, when I arrived home, she'd already gone to bed. A cold chicken salad was waiting for me on the breakfast bar in the kitchen. Just that. No note. Nothing. I went upstairs to wash, tried the bedroom door and found it locked. For the first time in our married life I'd been locked out of our bedroom. A sobering thought. A very hurtful act on her part. I could hear her moving about in the bedroom, and I knocked and called, but she refused to answer. God help me, I even pleaded with her to open the door and at least talk things over, but she refused to answer.

A ridiculous situation at our age. Childish. Beyond all reason, but in this mood she *is* beyond all reason.

I suppose, in the best Hollywood tradition (perhaps in the tradition of the heroes of her damned romantic novels) I should have broken down the door. Perhaps she expected me to. *Wanted* me to.

Not for me, I'm afraid. I am not a violent man. Not a destructive man. I am, I suspect, one of the anything-for-a-quiet-life types. A form of weakness, and I pay for it. I sometimes pay for it very dearly, but it is my nature and I can't alter.

A silly little rebellion on my part. I do not particularly like cold chicken salad, so I threw the meal into the dustbin, washed the plate then walked more than two miles to the nearest fish-and-chip shop. As I walked back home I ate the fish and chips from the paper. Maude would have been shocked. Mortified. It would, I am sure, have verified her long-held and not-so-secret opinion: that she made the mistake of marrying 'below' herself.

And yet I enjoyed that makeshift meal as I strolled home. It would be no exaggeration to say that, despite the miseries of the day, I felt happy and content. Alone. Content. Tasting simple, hot food and oblivious to the November nip in the air. Ridiculous. For a short time I forgot about Maude. I forgot about everything. I was hungry, and I was eating food I enjoyed and nothing else seemed to matter.

Remember that, Harry. The heart and the head. Important parts of the body. But when you're hungry (even though you don't realise that you are hungry) the stomach takes over, and all else is comparatively unimportant. All else is forgotten in the pleasure of food. Wisdom. The digestive system must never be under-rated.

And now, alas, I must make-do-and-mend for the coming night. Pride (what pride I have) prevents me from begging to be allowed to sleep in my own bedroom. An armchair, perhaps. The sofa. I suspect I am in for an uncomfortable night. I could use the guest bedroom, but that would reveal our stupidity to the cleaning woman. A marital spat. I don't want it round the village. She gossips. Therefore the sofa and everything cleared away before she arrives.

It is now past 3.15 am. (Strictly speaking, it is November the 3rd.) The discomfort of a sofa is only matched by the discomfort of an armchair which, in turn, is only matched by the discomfort of cushions on the hearthrug. I am deadly tired, but sleep will not come. My racing mind has combined with the unusual postures of my limbs to prevent rest.

I therefore record my thoughts (some of the thoughts which have tortured me) since I closed this diary only a few hours ago. I have at my elbow a good measure of whisky. I have loaded my favourite pipe and, despite the hour, the tobacco tastes good. I am seeking truth. Some sort of truth. Truth about Maude. Truth about myself. Truth about our marriage. Truth about *anything*.

15

Merely let it be the truth, and not some disguised excuse.

Facts.

I owe nobody a penny piece. No overdrafts. No mortgages. Every stick and stone, every nut and bolt, has been paid for. The printing firm I bought for a song, in the days when I was a cub reporter, is already earning itself a reputation for reliability and good-class work. The lesser publishing houses use the firm and are satisfied. The London-based giants are showing more than passing interest. This, in thirty years. With patience and a continuing eye for excellence, a good living could soon become a *very* good living. No partners other than my son, Harry. I made him a partner when he married. No directors other than Harry, Maude and myself. Maude (I make no secret of the fact) is a director for tax purposes only. She has yet to set foot in the firm. I do not fault her for that. The smell of printing ink can offend some people's nostrils. In any case she knows little, or nothing, about printing and is obviously not interested.

Conversely, Harry *does* show interest. Great interest. Without undue prodding on my part he has learned, and learned well. When the time comes for me to retire I already know that the firm will pass into safe and steady hands.

Fact Number One, then. No money problems. Equally, no prospect of future money problems.

Maude and myself. Leaving our marriage aside for a moment. Just *us*. Maude and John Duxbury. At the beginning. When we fell in love. I'd not long left grammar school and my father was a miner. Maude's father was a shopkeeper. A grocer. With *two* shops. Honesty above all . . . those two shops. They weren't small shops, but neither were they particularly large. Or even different. But two! In his eyes (in the eyes of Maude's mother) he was a provincial entrepreneur of no mean size. Like myself, Maude was an only child. She was spoiled. She was sent to a local 'private school', primarily to be taught to be a 'lady'. To her eternal credit, it did not completely ruin her. She could laugh. Indeed, if I remember anything about those days, it is her infectious giggle. She never admitted it (I think she was far too dutiful a daughter) but I think the ridiculous pomposity of both her parents tended to make her giggle sometimes. She was a delightful companion in

16

those days, and we had some wonderful times. She always led the way, but I was quite happy to follow.

Myself? By comparison, I was something of a dull dog. My sense of humour was very limited. (It still is, I fear.) I read a great deal. I cycled a great deal. Before meeting Maude I cycled alone. It was a fine bicycle. A half-drop-handle-barred Roger machine, with three-speed gear. No shorts or fancy windcheater. The only item of clothing peculiar to cycling were cycling shoes and only those because the toes were of hard leather and fitted the pedal-clips better than the toes of ordinary shoes. I had oilskin cape, leggings and sou'wester. I cared nothing about the weather. I was well protected. I learned the Yorkshire Dales on that excellent bicycle. I learned them and loved them. (I love them to this day.) So many times I have squatted in the grass of some verge, under the shelter of an oak or an elm and munched sandwiches and sipped hot tea from a Thermos, while the rain was pouring unheeded beyond my makeshift shelter. I was never wet, and rarely cold. I was always happy.

Shortly after I met her Maude bought a bicycle. I helped her to choose it. It, too, was a Roger. Thereafter, the two of us cycled the Dales together. Such innocence. Such happiness.

At that time I first read Hilton's *Goodbye Mister Chips* and, youthful fancy being what it is, I equated us with Chips and his young wife. (Although at that time we were not married.) In retrospect, and knowing what I know now, I realise the wisdom of Hilton in the writing of that story. The young wife died. What sort of story might it have been had Hilton allowed his young charmer to grow into embittered middle-age?

(I must be careful. I think the whisky is freeing thoughts and speculations which tend to cloud this attempt at reaching the truth!)

We married, against the expressed wishes of Maude's parents. She was over the age of consent, therefore the only thing they could do was try to talk her out of it. Try to talk *me* out of it. 'I'll be honest, John. I like you well enough – we both like you – but we expected Maude to marry into her own class.' It took me years, and more wisdom than I had at the time, to recognise that offensive remark as the prattling of a pompous, self-opinionated fool. Nevertheless, those ill-chosen words put steel into me. I worked, as I had never worked before, to make a success of that newly acquired printing works and, when that father-in-law of mine tottered on the brink of bankruptcy, when he had to sell one of his shops to pay his debts, I was (I admit it) secretly delighted.

Does that surprise you, Harry? That this non-personality father, whom I know you love but who, I suspect, you also despise a little, could (and still can) harbour such vindictive thoughts? Why not? If a man is weak in one thing he is weak in all things.

(I fear that these scribblings are becoming almost autobiographical. That was not the object. The object was truth.)

Our marriage. What on earth can a man say about his own marriage? What yardstick can he use? For all I know, other people's marriages parallel my own. They (like we) keep their squabblings behind closely locked doors. Secret squabblings. Secret humiliations. On the face of things they're happy. Moderately happy. At the very least, not openly *un*happy.

Tonight, when I couldn't sleep (when I'd been refused the comfort of my own bed) certain words kept entering my mind. 'Divorce'. 'Separation'. Ridiculous words. Utterly impossible words.

I come from a generation and from a background. Maude, too, comes from that same generation and from that same basic background. I think we were the people he had in mind when Shaw wrote *Pygmalion* and had Eliza's father rant on about 'middle-class morality'.

Other people divorce and separate. Not us. We are the 'respectable people'. We marry and *stay* married. However miserable, however pathetic our lives, we 'stick it out'. Why? God only knows. In this day and age, when simple humanitarian principles form the basis of divorce law, *we* are the masochistic idiots who ruin the only life we have in the sacred name of mock-'decency'. The sheer arrogance! The refusal to acknowledge even the possibility that we've made a mistake. The purile righteousness of it all. My God! We deserve every moment of misery we suffer.

Wrong! *Wrong*! WRONG!

The whisky, again. Damn the whisky. I should not have written

18

that. I love my wife. I *love* her. She is not perfect, but who is? How do I know she isn't suffering? Suffering more than I am? How do I know *she* hasn't toyed with the idea of divorce or separation? How do I know she hasn't cause? How do I *know*?

What man knows himself? Can understand himself? Can trace the source of feelings and thoughts which pass through his mind? Surely we all act a part. From the moment we speak. From the moment we can communicate. From the moment we 'want' something. A facade. A lie. A slightly different part for each person we know and for each person we meet. Even a different part for ourself, when we are alone. Each man an everlasting liar, an everlasting play-actor.

Therefore, what is our true self, and would we recognise it if we accidentally stumbled across it? Would we recognise it or would it be a stranger and, perhaps, not a very nice stranger?

I am coming to believe that nobody knows what 'truth' is. That in the final analsis 'truth' is little more than a firmly held opinion.

My God! Parlour philosophy at this hour of the morning.

So much for my search for truth. Bone-weariness superimposed upon a whisky-befuddled brain. I must sleep. I am too tired to write more. I must have *some* sleep before I start a new day.

WEDNESDAY, 3RD NOVEMBER

What a day!

Lack of sleep, marital problems and now trouble at the printing works.

Like any sensible employer, I pay good wages. Above average. Never less than three per cent above the nationally negotiated amount. It means a slimmer profit margin, but it also allows me to veto any suggestion of over-manning or ludicrous restrictive practices. I hold the firm opinion that the British working man is prepared, even eager, to do his best, if he is treated as a human being and an equal in the production of some end-product. Until two years ago we suffered no union trouble. I firmly (but politely) refused to run a 'closed shop' but, at the same time, I respected the right of any employee to join whichever union took his fancy.

Two years ago Evans joined the firm. A skilled operator. Credit where credit is due, he knew his job. But he was a born trouble-maker. Even Jim Jennings warned me. Dear old Jim. A craftsman of the old school, he came with the firm when I took the firm over. He calls himself a Marxist but, like no other extremist I know, he is very reasonable. I think the 'Marxist' tag is one he rather likes, but doesn't really know the meaning of. We have no officially elected leader of the shop-floor workers, but all the employees (less than twenty) are happy to let Jim be spokesman whenever they feel they have a grievance. I have no objection. It rarely happens, but when it does he talks as an equal and tries to see both sides. We have this in common. We both want the firm to prosper.

Evans had been with us little more than six months when Jim visited me in my office. I remember the exchange, word for word.

'You'll have to watch that new lad.'

(To Jim, any man less than sixty years old is a 'lad'. Anybody with less than ten years of service with the firm is 'new'.)

'Evans?' I guessed.

'He's stirring it up a bit.'

'In what way?'

'The roof leaks. Not much, but . . .'

'I didn't know that.'

'Not much, and only when it pisses down. It doesn't do any harm, and nobody has to stand under it.'

'What's Evans doing?' I asked.

'Yapping about "working conditions". "Positive action". You know what *that* means, with a silly bugger like him.'

'Strike action,' I sighed.

'If he can.' Jim nodded sadly. 'I'm not with him. But he's got one or two barmpots listening.'

'I'm obliged, Jim,' I thanked him.

'I'm not tittle-tattling.' I remember the scowl which went with the words. 'I just don't fancy standing on a bloody picket line for bugger-all at my time of life.'

The roof was repaired within forty-eight hours and the carpet was pulled from under Evans's feet, but during the last eighteen

20

months or so I've heard rumours (never from Jim) that Evans has spent much time insinuating that the firm is a sweat shop. That the reason we pay over-the-odds wages is because we expect each man to do two men's work. As I've heard it, it has had little effect, other than on half-a-dozen of the less-valued men. Therefore . . .

However. This morning . . .

Harry came into the office. It was after ten. I think not quite half-past. He looked angry enough for me to know that something had upset him.

'We have a thief,' he said without preamble. 'Evans is a thief.'

'They're all thieves.' I smiled and tried to soothe him. He'd spent the last two days stock-taking for the year-end. I waved him to a chair, and said, 'Perks, Harry. What's known as "natural wastage". A man works at a place like this. There are certain things he can use at home. A little here, a little there. It won't . . .'

'Three hundred pounds worth of stuff in the last month. He even brags about it. God alone knows how much before. That's a hell of a lot more than "natural wastage".'

He leaned forward in the chair and tossed a sheet of foolscap onto the desk. All itemised. All costed. Some things he could only have taken to sell elsewhere. Of what use is printer's ink in the average household?

I read the list carefully. 'You're sure?' I asked.

'I'm sure.'

'That it's Evans?'

'Some of the men have opened up. They're disgusted. They'll tell you. They'll sign statements.'

'Sign statements?' I didn't grasp the implication at first.

'He's a *thief*, dad.'

I nodded, then asked, 'Have you tackled him?'

'No. That's a job for the police.'

'Harry . . .' I had enough troubles. Still have. A police enquiry was something I didn't want. I said, 'I think he should be given a chance to explain. That, at least.'

'Dad, he's a rabble-rouser. A thief. What more do you . . .'

'I want him in here.'

'Dad, you're too damn soft. You . . .'

'I'm also your father. In addition, I'm the managing director of

21

this firm.' He needed reminding. It *was* my firm. Come to that, it was my family. Somebody needed reminding of *that*, too. I softened my tone a little, and said, 'My way, Harry. No bull-in-a-china-shop tactics. Get Evans in here. Quietly. Don't tell him why. And ask Jim to come, too.'

'Jim?' Poor Harry couldn't follow my reasoning.

'Evans will be opposing two directors,' I explained patiently.

'That won't have much effect on . . .'

'Two against one. That's not on. He needs somebody else. Somebody from the shop floor. Somebody prepared to speak his mind, if necessary.'

'Damn it, dad, we're not . . .'

'We're doing it *my* way. Evans and Jim Jennings. Then come back here. Give him a hearing. Listen to what Jim has to say. *Then*, if you must, express an opinion.'

Perhaps Harry is right. Perhaps I am too soft. Certainly Evans thought so. He denied everything. He accused me of setting a trap in order that I might have reason to sack him. He even threatened, towards the end.

'I'll have this bloody place closed, Duxbury. I'll have every bloody man in this . . .'

'Hold on!' Jim interrupted him and, by the look on his face, Jim was in no mood for polite conversation. He glared at Evans and said, 'Who the hell are *you*, when you're at home? Don't start trying to pull the wool over *my* eyes, lad. I'm not Mister Duxbury. I'm one of them that's watched you, and wondered where the hell it was going to stop. And I'll tell you another thing, lad, the only reason I haven't shopped you is because I'm not a gaffer's man. Never was. But, by hell, now you've been found out, I'll be the first in that witness box to make sure you get all you deserve.' The glare intensified. 'And as for closing this place down, just take heed. Just bloody-well try! Most of the lads in that shop know when they've a good job. And I'm one of 'em. If you as much as show your stupid face in that shop again, you'll risk six lace-holes up your arse . . . and my boot will be first to land. Don't forget, *I'm* a member of the union. So try tricks on those lines and the chapel knows next day.' He quietened a little, turned to me, and ended, 'He's yours now, Mister Duxbury. But we don't want him working with us any more.'

'I'll telephone the police.' Harry half-rose from his chair.

I rested a hand on the receiver and said, 'No.' Then to Evans, 'Collect your cards, Evans. We'll send what we owe in wages on to your home address. Don't ask for a reference . . . you won't get one. But if anybody rings, I'll tell them you know your job.'

There was a moment or two of squabbling. Harry was eager to send for the police, but he's young and hot-blooded. Given time, given experience, he'll learn that the shortest way out of trouble is always the best. I think Evans expected the police. I think he held me in contempt because I didn't call the police, despite his loud-mouth pleas of innocence. It was there in his eyes. He's that type of lout. Even Jim shook his head in puzzlement.

No matter. It's my way. I've rid the firm of Evans. That's enough.

This evening I moved my clothes – my suits, shirts, under-clothes, night-clothes, etc – into the guest bedroom. I made no secret of it. I did it slowly and deliberately, and not in a huff. All it needed was a word, a gesture, from Maude and I would happily have moved them all back into the master-bedroom. She ignored me, with that icy disdain women can adopt when they know they're in the wrong but wish to be thought to be in the right. It needed one word. Just one word. But from *her* . . . not from me! No apology. I count myself both old enough and experienced enough not to ask for even token grovelling. A single expression of sadness would have been enough.

Dammit, why should *I* always be the one to pocket my pride? Why must middle-aged women revert to the antics of stupid schoolgirls whenever their arrogance gets the better of their good manners? Why can't they ever be *wrong*?

At least I shall sleep tonight. The bed in the guest bedroom is very comfortable.

We seem to have fallen into a routine.

At least we are back to speaking to each other, but not man-and-wife conversation. There is a distance between us which shouldn't be there. We act towards, and speak to each other, like strangers in a hotel. Politely, but without real meaning.

A routine, then, instead of a marriage.

I rise long before she leaves her bed. Make my own small breakfast and am out of the house before the daily woman arrives. I take what mail is addressed to me to the office to read. If it needs answering, I answer it from the office. Mail addressed to either Maude or to both of us I leave on the hall table. What happens to it, after that, I have no idea. I am never told. I am not even handed letters to read. We have friends. We have relations (cousins, even aunts) and I sometimes recognise their handwriting on the envelopes. But I am denied knowledge of what they've had to say . . . and I'm damned if I'll ask!

Most of the evening I spend here in my study. Catching up on paperwork. Reading. Listening to my portable radio. This evening I listened to Alister Cooke giving an illustrated talk about jazz instruments. Tonight, the piano. Among others Fats Waller. Such a sad memory. Maude and I were crazy about him once. The best. The happiest. I still hold that opinion, but Maude . . .

Where *did* all the happiness go? As if we'd stored it in a leaking container, it seems to have just drained away. We have what once held it, but it's empty today. Such a waste. Such a waste of two lives. Where *did* it go? And why couldn't one of us see that it was going? Fats Waller once made me happy. Gloriously happy, just to listen to him. Now, he makes me sad. Dear God, life can be very cruel.

Don't let it happen, Harry. Keep a close watch. Don't *allow* it to happen. Work for it, fight for it. Anything! You have a good wife, a good marriage. The happiness we once had. Hang onto it, son.

24

That, above all else. Nothing is as important, but nothing is as fragile. When it goes, it's gone forever.

Time for bed. The guest bedroom. A 'guest' in my own home. It seems to sum everything up perfectly.

It is 2.30 am, and I am here, back again in my study. No sleep. I think the Fats Waller memories kept me awake. The memories and the might-have-beens.

No whisky this time. Instead, a beaker of drinking chocolate to accompany my pipe and these scribblings. And the never-ending questions. Why? Where did we go wrong? Whose fault has it been?

I talk to you, Harry, because I have nobody else to whom I can talk. More than that. I can't even talk to you, face-to-face. Only in this diary-of-a-sorts, and only with the near-certain knowledge that you will read these words when I am well past caring.

Our marriage is not smashed. Let that be clear. In many ways, it may no longer exist, but I could no more leave your mother than I could chop off one of my own limbs. Stupid. Ridiculous. But to say otherwise would not be honest. We need each other. How to put it? It starts with a love-relationship, then moves onto what can only be described as a love-hate-relationship, then the hatred grows and it ends with a hate-relationship. But the *relationship* remains. The bond never loosens. The knowledge that the other is there must remain until death. Apart, I would spend all my days worrying about her. I think she would spend her days worrying about me. Yet, together, we don't seem to give a damn.

The contradiction is outrageous. Beyond understanding. The only certain thing is that it is *there*.

I am convinced that the human animal must be . . .

WEDNESDAY, 10TH NOVEMBER

I wonder what the human animal must be?

In the small hours of morning the mind explores strange paths. For the life of me I can't remember what the end of that sentence was going to be. What earth-shattering truth I intended to pen.

25

Just that I heard the sound of movement and popped this diary out of sight.

Maude tapped on the door and entered my study. She said she'd heard somebody downstairs and had come to investigate. Burglars, perhaps? I pretended to believe. (Knowing Maude, as I do, the last thing she would have done, had she *really* taken the possibility of burglars seriously, would have been to leave the bedroom.) I made some sort of apology and explained that I hadn't been able to sleep.

'Isn't the guest bed comfortable?'

'Oh, yes. Very comfortable.' I forced a smile, and added, 'Fats Waller.'

'Fats Waller?'

'They played some of his records on the radio earlier this evening. Memories. I couldn't sleep for memories.'

'Oh!'

I placed my pipe in the ash-tray. She doesn't like pipes. That's why I only smoke a pipe in my study when at home.

'Chocolate?' I touched my half-empty beaker. 'I could do with some more. Shall I make two?'

'Please.'

'In the kitchen?' I suggested. 'It's warmer.'

'All right.'

Strange what an effort it took. We both knew the quarrel was over. It had run its course. They always do. But they never come to an abrupt end. They taper off into nothingness. There is no sudden kiss-and-make-up as in fiction. (Damn it, when *did* we last kiss?) Instead, there is a slow lowering of weapons. The 'weapons', of course, being either hurtful words or equally hurtful silences. A slow lowering. A gradual attempt at communication. Difficult, at first. But very slowly it becomes easier.

Take the stilted conversation in the kitchen, as we sipped hot chocolate.

'Are you sure that bed in the guest bedroom is comfortable?'

'Yes, quite comfortable.'

'I mean, if it's not as comfortable as your own bed.'

'I – er – I manage.'

'Just don't be stubborn. That's what I'm saying.'

26

'I try not to be stubborn, dear. Is the chocolate all right?'

'Yes. Very nice. Just that . . . your own bed's there, if you want it.'

'If you – y'know – want me to sleep in the main bedroom.'

'That's up to you, of course.'

'Yes, I know.' (How careful we must be not to push things along too quickly.) 'It's just that you've complained that I snore, sometimes.'

'Not often.'

'I don't want to disturb you.'

'It doesn't happen very often.'

(We are, you will note, both deliberately avoiding the *real* cause of the quarrel. The cracked cup in the café. The fact that I occasionally snore is a handy, ready-made peg upon which to drape this tiptoeing towards friendship. In a roundabout way, it puts Maude in the right. It makes *me* the reason for the shift in bedrooms.)

'It's up to you,' she said.

'No. I'll leave it to you. You decide.'

'If we do have guests, it *will* look rather silly.'

'Yes. I suppose so.'

When I arrived from the office this evening she had moved all my things back to the master bedroom. Neither of us said anything. It was neither a victory nor a defeat.

The mundane stuff of which marriages are made, I suppose. Not exactly 'give and take'. Rather a slow (almost unwilling) capitulation on both sides. A meeting-in-the-middle because we both feel aggrieved, and at the same time both feel a little foolish.

A poor foundation for a marriage, but the best we have. If not respect for the other, at least self-respect.

MONDAY, 15TH NOVEMBER

Today could be a very important day for the firm. Today and tomorrow. A make-or-break period.

A telephone call from one of the major London publishing houses. Could we discuss the printing of at least part of their list? A trial

27

period? A meeting with one of the directors, perhaps? Person-to-person, in order that it be explained exactly what was required, and whether the firm was capable of meeting certain deadlines and fulfilling certain contractual requirements.

Tomorrow? Would that be convenient?

Unfortunately, the director has a very heavy schedule and can't travel north and back in a day, and still have sufficient time to go into the necessary details with me. Saffron Walden? He could meet me at the Saffron Hotel at (say) half-past-six, we could discuss the project over dinner, then he could return to London later that night. Would that be convenient?

Would it be convenient!

It *had* to be convenient. No matter that Saffron Walden was more than two-thirds of the distance to London. No matter that London itself would have been *more* convenient (a local train from Harrogate to Leeds, then a high-speed train to King's Cross) if the director preferred Saffron Walden, Saffron Walden it would be. The A1 south, then the A14 to Saffron Walden. Three hours. Four hours at the most.

I checked the hotel in *Egon Ronay*, telephoned, booked a room for tomorrow night and booked early dinner for two at as secluded a table as they could provide. It sounded a good hotel. The lady answering my call tentatively suggested that dinner might be served in my room, but I declined. I wanted that contract. On the other hand, I didn't know the man I was to meet, and I didn't want to give the impression of lickspittle or even super-affluence. We were a successful firm. A good firm. We were prepared to be inconvenienced for the sake of good customers. But there was a subtle limit and, to go beyond that limit might suggest that we were prepared to tout.

Harry was as delighted as I was. I think he wanted to go or, at least, go with me. But that is impossible. One of us must stay at the office and keep a weather eye on the firm. Nevertheless, he *was* delighted. Not once have I regretted making him a director of the firm.

Maude, I'm afraid, is less than delighted. She dislikes the idea of spending a night alone in the house. Somebody (her own words) might break in and attack her. In God's name, why? Why *should* anybody? Who is likely to know? What is more, we have strong doors, firm windows and a perfectly good external burglar alarm.

'Why can't I come with you?'

'My dear, this is a business trip. A very important business trip. It's not a vacation.'

'You mean I'll be in the way.'

'No. Of course you won't be in the way.'

'In that case, why can't . . .'

'But I don't know the man I'm to meet. Some men don't like talking business with wives present.'

'I can look round the town.'

'We don't meet until early evening. Until after dark.'

'I needn't sit at the same table.'

'Don't be silly. It's a business meeting, not a spy novel.'

'I don't like staying here alone.'

'I'll ring Harry. They'll come and spend the night here.'

'Don't you dare!'

'Why not?'

'They'll think I'm frightened. That I'm a coward.'

'You *are* frightened.'

'That doesn't mean . . .'

'For Heaven's sake, he's our son.'

'You don't understand *anything*, do you? You don't understand a *thing*.'

And that, if nothing else, is the truth. To be frightened (especially if you're a woman) is nothing to be ashamed of. But there are answers and, in our case, the obvious answer was to ask Harry and Ben over for the night. And yet the suggestion seemed tantamount to an insult.

She seems to grow more difficult each day. This has been an important day. Possibly even a milestone in our business life. But that means nothing to her. I feel another quarrel brewing. No, that's wrong. Life with Maude is one long quarrel. What I feel is one more growing crescendo in that quarrel. One more impossible period.

'The rough with the smooth'. That's what they say. My God! I wonder when the smooth part is likely to arrive?

This entry must be made. I owe it to Harry. This diary is meant to be read by Harry. By my son, and by nobody else. I fear he looks upon his father as something of a failure. Not in all things, I hope. Not a complete failure in business, for example. But in some things. In most things. He may be right (I tend to think he *is* right) but I will not make excuses. No excuses! Merely explanations. What has happened and, if I can fathom the reasons, why it happened. Why I think it happened.

Judge me carefully, Harry. Judge me by *my* yardstick, not your own.

Yesterday morning I rose early, bathed, dressed and was away before Maude was even awake. I think the excitement had something to do with it, but in addition I'd planned the day carefully. It was probably wrong to go and not even wake her, but it didn't seem wrong at the time. It seemed natural enough to let her sleep undisturbed.

I wanted to be away and on the A1 before the bulk of the goods vehicles claimed the carriageways. I'd estimated that, once south of Doncaster, much of the heavy stuff would have turned off and onto the motorways. That the hundred miles or so of the A1 from Doncaster to Huntingdon would be comparatively easy driving.

It was a good morning. Shortly after dawn when I set off. That half-hour drive along the country lanes to the A1 was well worth the early rise. There was a mist. Nothing to cause trouble or difficult driving. A light November mist. Grey. Almost white. It seemed to be clinging to the trees. To the almost leafless branches. It gave a 'Japanese print' effect to the whole countryside. Very beautiful. If the occasion arises we must try for a similar effect in the line drawings of some book. A wraith-like effect. I think it could be achieved without colour. Just a minimum of lines. A mere suggestion of a landscape, as if seen through fine muslin.

I was wrong about the A1. The heavy vehicles were there in

force. They have schedules to keep, of course. I realise that. But I find the drivers are not like those of some few years back. More reckless. Less considerate. They seem younger, too. Younger and more brash. I suspect they know the power they control. Only a lunatic motorist would insist upon right of way when opposed by a juggernaut lorry.

South of Doncaster things eased a little, as I thought they would. People complain of motorways. The environmentalists and their ilk. But at least they hive off much of the traffic weight. They are not *meant* to be beautiful. They are functional. If anything, they are meant to allow lesser roads to *keep* their beauty. To some degree, they succeed.

I drove easily. Carefully. I was in no great hurry. That's why I gave myself far more time than was necessary. To stop occasionally. To pull into a lay-by, wind down the window and enjoy a pipe of tobacco. Plan what I was going to say to this director. The limits of any agreement we could afford. I had a briefcase filled with samples. Much of it our standard output, but also a selection of some of our speciality stuff. Not that I expected him to want any of *that*. But at least it would give him proof of our capabilities. The truth is, I was a little like a schoolboy hours away from an important exam. I knew I could do it. Knew I had all the possible 'answers' ready. But as with the schoolboy I was nervous. A sort of 'exam nerves'. It was important. Very important. The firm has gone as far as it ever can go without the custom of some major publishing house. But with that custom, and if with that custom we could really make a name for ourselves, the future is ours. Yours and mine. Built up from almost nothing. We could . . .

I dream. It's a possible dream. It *could* come true. But the recording of my dreams is not the object of this entry.

I'd had no breakfast. Only a quick cup of instant coffee and, once on my way, I looked out for somewhere to have a snack. There is a village called Marston. On the left, as you travel south along the A1. Just north of the Grantham turn-off. It's sign-posted. I'd dawdled long enough for it to be opening time by the time I reached the road leading to Marston. There's a pub there. On the right as you get into the village from the A1. I don't know its name. I hadn't the wit to notice. But if you're ever in that area, Harry, and you want a meal or a bar snack, they cater well and at a very reasonable price. Much better than the stuff they serve at the roadside cafes.

I broke my journey there. Spent about an hour. Despite what I'd said to Maude it *was* a vacation . . . of a sort.

I had an important meeting ahead of me and yet I felt happy. Free. The truth? I was beyond the restrictive complaints of Maude. For a time (for a single day) I was my own man. It was a little like throwing off a straitjacket. A little like being young again. Oh yes, for a short time, as I held a pint of good beer in one hand, my pipe in the other, and chatted away to one of the locals, I felt an underlying feeling of guilt. Maude would not have approved. To talk freely with complete strangers. To laugh aloud at a mildly bawdy joke. To quaff good ale, and smack my lips at the taste. To stand at a bar and eat from a plate without a napkin. Oh, my word! If she could only have *seen* me. 'The mood' would have lasted for days. Probably weeks.

That vague feeling of guilt didn't last for long, I fear. For the first time in years I was tasting innocent enjoyment. Enjoyment! I'd almost forgotten what it felt like. The guilt-feeling lasted no time at all.

I reached the Saffron Hotel by mid-afternoon. It is on the left as you drive along the town's main street from the north. A picturesque hotel, suited to a picturesque little town. It even has a tiny courtyard.

As you know, I have always had an aversion to hotels which claim to provide 'home-from-home' comforts. To me a most off-putting suggestion. I go on holiday, I stay at a hotel, the last thing I want is to feel I'm still at home. I pay to be pandered to a little. I demand minor luxuries. Not too much, I hope, but at least I want to know that I'm *not* at home. That there are people there to give cheerful service over and above my normal way of life.

The Saffron Hotel meets my requirements perfectly.

My bedroom was quite delightful. Clean, newly decorated in a pleasant colour scheme. A very comfortable bed. A *double* bed. It not being in season, few of the eighteen bedrooms were occupied and, as she opened the bedroom door for me, the pleasant lady who'd shown me to the room said, 'A double bed, Mr Duxbury.

You'll be able to stretch out to your heart's content.' The adjoining bathroom, with both bath and shower, lacked nothing. The hot water was *really* hot and, as I cleaned off the grime and weariness of travel, I silently congratulated whoever it was who'd recommended this particular hotel.

Downstairs, after having bathed and changed, I discovered that the hotel must have been the rendezvous of flying men during World War II. Fighters and bombers, at a guess. Two good prints held pride of place on the walls of the lounge. A Lancaster bomber and a Spitfire fighter. The walls also held framed photographs of groups of young men in flying gear. Young men who are now either dead or old men. It didn't take much guesswork to realise that The Saffron Hotel had once been the meeting place favoured by the RAF on their off-duty periods. Certain relics of those days hung on the walls. No doubt treasured relics. I found myself wondering which bomber group, which fighter squadron, was stationed within easy distance of the town.

A nice hotel. A hotel with charm. With character; with its own cosy 'atmosphere'. The feeling of being on holiday increased.

I checked that the dinner was ordered, called at the reception desk and told them I was expecting a guest then bought a glass of 'real ale' and sat down in a corner of the lounge to wait.

I'd been there about half-an-hour, perhaps less, when the woman . . .

Harry, before I write another word, certain things need saying. It wasn't a pick-up. Not on my part. Not on her part. She was no tart out for a quick and cheap evening out. Had you met her your reaction would have been the same as mine. Your assessment the same. A middle-class, respectable woman of moderate means. Neatly dressed. Quietly mannered. In her late-forties or thereabouts. A little tall perhaps. But trim and with a neat figure which she most certainly did not flaunt.

She carried her gin and lime from the bar counter to the corner table at which I was sitting and hesitated (truly, she *hesitated*) before asking whether she might share the table.

'I dislike standing at the bar, and most of the other tables seem to be taken up by groups who might look upon my presence as an intrusion.'

33

A reasonable request. A perfectly valid reason for making the request. And why should we not exchange small-talk? We were each alone, albeit not lonely. We came from a similar class level. To just sit at the table and ignore each other would have been ill-mannered, to say the least.

I mentioned how much I liked the hotel, and that I had an appointment with a business colleague at dinner.

She volunteered the information that she was travelling to Hastings to visit her married daughter. That, so far, she'd driven from Newcastle.

'I usually break my journey at Cambridge, but a friend recommended this place. I must admit, I'm very much impressed.'

That sort of talk. The conversation of polite, middle-aged people thrown together by chance. From the start, we were at ease with each other. Neither of us tried to impress. There was no need. We talked, quietly and politely, until the arrival of the London-based director, then I took my leave and he and I went into the dining room for our meal.

You know the outcome of that meeting. We have a chance (a good chance, I think) of landing the biggest contract the firm has had so far. But he was a very 'busy' man. He refused a drink before dinner, virtually gobbled the food as it was placed before him and was obviously in a tearing hurry to get back to London. However, he was impressed by the 'samples', assured me that he would have no difficulty in convincing his fellow-directors that a change of printer would be a good thing, then hared off back to London by nine o'clock.

During dinner I had noticed the woman eating alone in the dining room. A couple of times she'd caught my eye and half-smiled. As if in encouragement. As if wishing me luck. Nothing more. No hint of coquettishness.

The question, then, which must be asked. The question I know *you* will ask when you read this entry. How did we end up in bed together? The circumstances via which, for the first time, I broke my marriage vows? Come to that, why record it? Why not allow it to remain a secret?

Harry, I love you. I love you as much as any father has ever loved his son. More than that, however. I wish you to respect me, but not because convention *expects* you to respect me. I wish you to respect me (perhaps respect my memory) because I have earned that respect. Warts and all. I make no claim to be perfect, but I insist that you be told my imperfections by me. Not second-hand. They remain imperfections, but at least they are told by the one person who knows the truth.

And, having said that, how to make you understand?

It was nine o'clock, remember. About nine o'clock. The bar had filled with local customers. Not rowdy, but boisterous. Young people, laughing and joking, with modern pop music as a background. It's what people like these days. What they want. It's what the management of a hotel must provide. I blame nobody. Only my own taste, my own timidity and the fact that a surfeit of noise (even happy noise) is something I dislike.

She was sitting alone in an armchair not far from the table we'd shared before dinner. Sipping her gin and lime. Looking vaguely uncomfortable. The hint of a frown on her face. I took an empty stool and joined her. She seemed pleased to have somebody to talk to, and asked about the business appointment. A polite remark. Not nosey in any way. Just something to say. To start a conversation.

'As well as can be expected,' I said.

'Young people.' She glanced at the crowded bar and smiled. 'They know how to enjoy themselves.'

'Very harmless,' I observed, then added, 'But not of my generation. Not my sort of music.'

'Nor mine.' She glanced at her watch. 'There's an Alan Bennett play on at half-past-nine. I think I'll go and watch it.'

'Er . . .'

'On television. I have one in my bedroom.'

'Oh, yes. So have I.'

'More in my line than this.' She smiled again.

'Mine, too.' I ventured an opinion. 'I think *View Across The Bay* was his best.' Then, I added, hastily, 'I haven't seen them all, of course.'

'From Leeds,' she said.

'Who?'

'Alan Bennett. He catches the Northern turn of phrase

35

perfectly.'

'Oh – er – yes.'

'Funny, and yet with pathos. Always that underlying pathos. I think he must be a sad person. Sad, but very kind.'

'Possibly,' I agreed. Then, seeing her glass was almost empty, said, 'May I buy you a drink?'

'No, it's quite . . .' Then she closed her mouth, smiled again, and said, 'Yes. Why not? Gin and lime, please. I'll take it up to my room. Drink it while I watch the play.' She hesitated. Nor was it a false hesitation. She chewed her lower lip, as if undecided for a moment, then almost blurted, 'Why not join me?'

'What?'

'Watching the play. Unless, of course you'd rather stay down . . .'

'No. That's a very nice idea. And kind of you. I think I will. I'll get the drinks, then we can go and settle down with Alan Bennett.'

Understand me, the conversation was as innocent as I've recorded it. No innuendoes. No unspoken promises. Two people, of an age, who didn't quite 'fit in' with modern merrymaking. And there was a good play on TV . . . so why not watch it together?

Dammit, as innocent as *that*! A double whisky, topped up with water. A gin and lime. Nor did we make a secret of leaving the room together. We even wished the receptionist 'Goodnight'. Both of us. And she, in turn, returned the pleasantry.

We watched the play. Two armchairs. She chose one. I settled into the other. We watched the play, and I doubt whether we spoke more than half-a-dozen words while it was being shown. I sipped my whisky. She sipped her gin and lime. We really *had* come to the bedroom to watch a good television play. That and nothing more.

When the play was over she switched off the set and returned to her chair. She lighted a cigarette and I asked her permission to smoke my pipe.

'Certainly. My husband used to smoke a pipe.'

'Your husband?' It was still small-talk. A sort of rebound of her remark.

'He died three years ago.'

'I'm sorry.'

'Time dulls the pain.'

36

The impression was that she'd loved her husband. No, more than an impression. A certainty. Her tone. The hint of once-upon-a-time heartbreak which can't be imitated.

'Are you married?' she asked.

'Oh, yes. I have a married son. Harry.'

'As happily married as I was, I hope.'

'Harry?'

'No . . . you. Both of you.'

'Oh, yes. I'm happily married. Her name's Maude.'

I said it, and meant it. With all my heart, I meant it. It was true because, at that moment, I *wanted* it to be true. Not the past tense. Not that I'd *once* been happily married, but that I still was. That the joy of those first years was still present. Believe that, Harry. Believe that, if you believe nothing else. I did not sully the name of your mother by playing the 'misunderstanding wife' ploy. Indeed, at that moment, there was no ploy at all. A pleasant evening was drawing to a close. We were chatting the last few moments away. That's what it was. That and nothing more.

The subject-matter of that empty chat? To be honest, I can't remember. The weather? Perhaps. It was a cold night outside, although the excellent central heating system kept the hotel cosy and warm. The play we'd just watched? It's possible. Bennett's plays are given to encouraging conversation and the expressing of opinion. The hotel itself? Perhaps so. Indeed, I rather think we must have mentioned the hotel.

She asked, 'What's your room like?'

'Like this.' I looked around the room for the first time. 'The twin of this, in fact.'

I recall, I was still sitting in the armchair, finishing what was left of the tobacco in my pipe. She was up. Behind me. I'm not sure, but I think she was turning down the top cover of the bed. Like the one in my own room, a double bed.

In what was little more than a whisper, she said, 'Why go back?'

There was a slight tremble in the question. As if the asking of it had taken courage.

I didn't know how to react. It was so sudden. So unexpected. I didn't say anything.

'You heard me?' she breathed.

37

'Yes.'

'Have I . . . have I shocked you?'

'Surprised, perhaps. Not shocked.'

'Well?'

'I'm . . .' I swallowed. I daren't turn in my chair. 'I'm a respectably married man.'

'I'm a respectable widow,' she said, quietly. 'We – y'know – just happen to be alone.'

'Do you . . .' The question took some asking. 'Do you want me to stay?'

'I wouldn't have made the suggestion.'

'No. Of course not.'

'But both of us. Not just me. *Both* of us.'

I remember saying, 'Thank you,' and it almost came out like a sigh. Like a sigh of relief.

Therefore, no pick-up, Harry. I've tried to put it down exactly as it happened. *Exactly*. It sort of crept up on us. It just happened. No pick-up. No slam-bang-thank-you-ma'am technique of a generation brought up to believe that promiscuity is theirs by right. Middle-aged people, probably just easing their way past the prime of life. Nor was it a one-last-fling situation. There was too much shyness, too much breathless hesitancy, in the initial approach.

But, having decided, there was no mock-modesty. Age still has its compensations. There was no teenage coyness.

We showered. She first. I remember the cleanliness of her underclothes. A strange thing to remember, but important at the time. Stained underclothes would have revolted me, I think. But they weren't. Silk. Pale pink silk, and immaculate. Nor was there a girdle or a corset. Her stomach muscles were firm enough to hold her erect. Statuesque. That is the only word to describe her. Statuesque and, despite her age, beautifully proportioned. She'd had at least one child (the daughter she was on her way to visit) but she'd looked after her body. Those breasts! Firm, and so much like crystal goblets I half expected them to ring when the jets of the shower struck them.

Thereafter we made love. Not lust. We weren't *in* love. I didn't love her, nor did she love me, but despite this it was not mere carnality. Love then, not lust. It *is* possible, Harry. It is possible

38

and, when it is possible, it is delightful. No inhibitions. She knew techniques new to me. She knew things Maude will never know. Four times, and each time a little better than the time before. Odd. I felt a pride in myself. That I was still man enough. That I was still able . . . and happy.

At a little after four o'clock I collected my clothes, returned to my own room and remembered until I fell asleep.

I awoke and dressed just in time for breakfast. She'd gone. She'd woken early, breakfasted and had left for Hastings before I sat down to breakfast.

I don't even know her name.

This morning, before I left for home, I wandered around the Saffron Walden shops seeking a gift for Maude. I chose a silk headscarf. Pure silk. Hand-painted. Expensive.

A conscience-gift, you think? I wouldn't agree. I'd have bought her something, anyway. Probably the same thing. In any case, I didn't feel guilty. I was curiously happy. Free. If I had sadness, it was only because I hadn't seen the woman to thank her and wish her a safe journey. But *guilt*? Not at all.

I arrived home late this afternoon. Maude liked the gift. So, we're all happy . . . aren't we?

And so to bed. It's been a long day, and this entry has taken longer than usual to write. But carefully. Every word weighed before written. Because I want you to know, Harry. I want you to know *exactly* what happened, and how it happened. From me, not second-hand should it ever come to light. How it happened, and how it might have happened to any other man, and without making the woman a whore or the man a womanizer.

One must presume that to follow a person, without that person being aware of the fact is not easy. Even when the person being followed has no reason to even suspect that he is being followed. I suppose it can be done. I know little of these things, but common sense insists that (say) police surveillance is possible. Given the man-power, given the equipment, given enough vehicles to ring enough changes. It *must* be possible.

But one man, and always the same man, and always the same car!

I became aware of him yesterday. On my way back to the office after lunch. I stopped a couple of times, perhaps three times, to look in shop windows. I was seeking Christmas presents. Had I not been, I would not have stopped, and I might not have spotted him. As it was, each time I stopped, *he* stopped. Usually about three shops away. I might not even have noticed him then had not one of the windows he chose been that of a dry-cleaning establishment. Why, in God's name, stare into a dry-cleaners? To make sure, I varied my pace a little and returned to the office via streets and alleys which doubled the length of my journey. As I rounded each corner, I glanced back. He was always there. At the office, I hurried to the window and peeped out. He was climbing into a Fiesta parked at a meter less than fifty yards from the works entrance. The Fiesta was still there when I left for home, and it travelled behind me until I turned off into the country lanes.

A podgy man. Not very tall. Moderately well-dressed in a dark brown suit. Clean-shaven. Wearing spectacles. He carried a folded mac over one arm.

That much I noticed. That, and the make and colour of the car, but not its number. I am not, I fear, too observant.

I didn't mention it to Maude. The thought crossed my mind that he might be a thief. A housebreaker, perhaps. With ambitions on either the works or the house. A possibility, perhaps, but only a bare possibility. How do breakers work? How do they 'case a joint' . . . to use their own ridiculous slang. Surely not so openly. Not so obviously. That's why I didn't mention the incident. Maude tends towards timidity. I didn't want to frighten her without reasonable cause. Nevertheless, I checked the doors and windows of the firm before I left, and I did the same at home, before I went to bed.

I pondered on it before I went to sleep. If not the firm, if not the house, what then? Me? Was I being examined for some future attack, perhaps? A mugging?

It wasn't a pleasant thought, but at the same time the man hadn't *looked* like a mugger. Assuming, of course, that muggers *have* a 'look'. To be on the safe side, I took a stout walking-stick with me to the office this morning. I parked the car well inside the firm's boundary wall. Checked that every door and window was locked. Hurried into the office and was in time to spot our friend feeding coins into the meter next to the one he used yesterday.

This lunch time, I decided to bottom the thing.

I set off from the office, made a quick check that he was following, then turned left instead of right and, without giving the impression of hurry or panic, strolled into the police station just along the road. As you are aware (and because we print tickets and posters for the annual Police Ball, etc.) they know us both, and I had no difficulty in arousing interest. I wasn't treated as a crank. A plain clothes officer nipped outside, having been given a description and, within minutes, our friend was in an interview room, with myself and a uniformed sergeant, being required to answer very pertinent questions.

He wasn't a criminal. Quite the opposite, in fact, although the sergeant treated him as something lower than any criminal!

His name is of no importance, but he was a private detective. Not a very successful one, I venture to suggest. A one-man 'private investigator' business, and he'd been paid (and was still being paid) to follow me and keep notes of my movements. Maude was footing the bill.

I was shocked. I asked him why, and he said that Maude had information that I had a woman somewhere. A woman I was having an affair with. He didn't know the name or the address of the woman, but (or so he'd been told) I met her regularly (usually at lunch times) and we had some trysting spot where, presumably, we were having this imaginary affair.

Shocks really can render you speechless. Momentarily, at least. That or create a raging anger capable of bringing about murder. As far as I was concerned, it was a combination of the two. I can only thank God that Maude wasn't within reach.

For a split second the Saffron Walden episode sprang to mind, but as this so-called private detective blurted out his tale, it became very obvious that, whatever Maude had in mind, it wasn't *that*. It was too recent. It had to do with somewhere, or somebody, here within easy distance of the office.

The sergeant (policemen being what they are) gave me a distinctively old-fashioned look. Maybe I *was* ramming away on the side. Maybe my wife *had* cause for suspicion. Maybe this snivelling little man *had* good reason for following me. I could read it in that look. That we're-all-men-of-the-world expression. And that, too, added to my anger.

'No more.' I almost choked on the words, as I spoke to the miserable creature in the pay of Maude. 'There must *be* a way of stopping you from following me. The police. If not the police, some sort of civil action. But it's going to *be* stopped. By God, yes! If the sergeant can't help me, I go straight from here to my solicitor's office. But, whatever it costs, you're going to be crushed, little man. If possible, you're going to be destroyed.'

I meant it, too. At that moment the target for my rage was this private detective character, and I let fly as I can never remember having let fly before. It scared him. It was *meant* to scare him. However much Maude was paying him it wasn't worth what *I* was prepared to make it cost him. I know I raged at him, threatened him, without cease for all of three minutes or thereabouts. Nor was I bluffing. And he knew that, too.

The sergeant touched my arm, and said, 'Take it easy, Mr Duxbury. Leave this little lot to me.' He turned to the man and in a cold voice said, 'You get the message?'

The man nodded. I think he was too frightened to speak.

'Loud and clear?'

Again the man nodded.

The sergeant said, 'If you want summonses – enough summonses to wallpaper a bedroom – let me find you following Mr Duxbury or anybody else. I'll have you lad. I'll have you by the short and curlies until you're screaming for mercy. Obstruction. Spitting on the pavement. Conduct likely to cause a breach of the peace. Depositing litter. You name it, lad. It'll be there. I'll make the bloody offences up, if necessary. You have a car?'

The man nodded again.

'Champion. I'll take that bloody car to pieces, I'll find more motoring offences than you ever dreamed existed. Tyres, horn, steering, lights, brakes . . . the whole bloody issue. And that before you even start the engine! I'll make that damn car cost you a hundred quid a week in fines alone.' He paused, then ended, 'You do get the gist, I hope?'

'I – I won't,' stammered the man.

'You won't *what*?'

'I won't follow him. I'll – I'll drop the case. Honest.'

'You never *had* a case. Now . . . out! Before I think up something to book you for before you even leave.'

The man hurried out of the room. The sergeant grinned a wicked grin, but I couldn't return the smile. I walked back to the office in something of a haze. I was still boiling with rage. I couldn't even trust myself on the shop floor. Some tiny little thing would have triggered off an explosion beyond all reason. For some hours, I think I was a little mad.

This evening, when I arrived home . . .

WEDNESDAY, 24TH NOVEMBER

Yesterday (last night) I was unable to finish the entry. I was far too emotionally disturbed. I'm sorry, Harry, but again we must face the truth. I am not a violent man. Anger (the degree of anger I felt last night) is something beyond my normal experience. However, it must be told, and tonight I feel better able to set things down as they happened and, hopefully, without exaggeration.

Yesterday evening when I arrived home, I was looking for signs.

43

A look, perhaps. A turn of phrase. Something via which I could judge exactly what Maude was up to.

Because I was looking, I found them. A sideways glance when she thought I wasn't watching. An emphasis on a word in an otherwise innocent remark, which gave that remark another meaning. A suggestive, dirty meaning. My temper was still at boiling point, but I controlled it (with some difficulty) until we'd eaten then, because there seemed no easy way to approach the subject, I tackled it head-on.

'A ridiculously inept man has been following me for two days,' I said bluntly. 'Possibly more than two days. I wouldn't know. A private detective of all things. He tells me he's been employed by you.'

It caught her unawares and for the moment she didn't answer. Just sat there, opening and closing her mouth.

'Something about another woman,' I continued in a hard voice. 'A fancy piece. His job was to report what he found back to you.'

'I – I don't know what you're . . .'

'Don't compound the damn thing by lying to me.' I think I shouted the words. 'I've had him in a police station. Questioned by a police sergeant. He's a terrified man. He has reason to be terrified. All I want from *you* is the answer to one question. *Why?*'

'It's . . .' She seemed unable to speak. She went to the sideboard, opened her handbag and handed me a folded sheet still in its grubby little envelope. I unfolded the sheet and read what was scrawled across it. *Watch that old goat you are married to missus. He has a young bird in tow. He sees her at lunch times. They have fun together where nobody can see them. I thought you ought to know. A Well Wisher.*

I examined the envelope. It was stamped, and franked at a city collection point on November 20th. Last Saturday. I examined the writing, both on the envelope and the letter.

I recall the disgust with which I spoke the one word, 'Evans.'

Credit where due, she waited. I felt some of the anger evaporate, then told her all she needed to know.

'I sacked him recently. Stealing. This is his way of getting back at me.'

'You're sure?' She didn't sound quite convinced.

'Woman,' I snapped, 'I'm not a fool. Nor is the man who wrote

44

this garbage. Short and to the point. No mis-spelt words. Just enough to cause trouble, but nothing specific. And I can recognise the handwriting. Dammit, he *wants* me to know.'

'I don't see why . . .'

'You're the fool!' I stormed. 'Not me. Not him. You! You believed this filth. My God, he knows you better than you know yourself.'

'If you're not . . .'

'*If* I'm not?' I came as near to hitting her as I'll ever come. 'You stupid, dirty-minded bitch. Do you still have doubts? Harry there in the works. Our own son? Would I? *Could* I?'

'No. I – I suppose . . .'

'What sort of damned imagination have you got? What sort of dirty pictures flash across that mind of yours?' I was furious. I have since reached the unhappy conclusion that secret guilt can fire indignation at wrongful accusation. That Saffron Walden episode was too recent not to have had *some* effect. For whatever reason, I stormed on. 'This filth. This outrageous and unfounded accusation. In God's name, haven't you even heard of "poison letters"? Am I so despicable that you immediately believe *any* accusation? Without even having the sense to tell me? A "private detective", for Heaven's sake. A cheap, keyhole-peeping snooper. A . . .'

No, I won't go on. Suffice to say that the tirade, although perhaps justified, went on too long. Far too long. I wanted to stop, but couldn't. I wanted the ridiculous farce to end, but found it to be too easy a vehicle to ride. Dammit, I wanted to hurt her. I'd *been* hurt. Too many times and over too long a period. I suppose it can be said that I required my pound of flesh. For once, *I* held the whip and (ashamed though I am to admit it) I got perverse pleasure from wielding it.

Harry, why do people hurt each other so much? Why do they get *pleasure* from hurting each other? I don't mean 'happy' pleasure. But nevertheless a kind of pleasure. A 'righteous' pleasure. Why? People who supposedly love each other. Who, at the very least, should *respect* each other. Grown people. Adults, with a life-time of experience to draw upon. Doesn't that experience count for *anything*? Eventually, a halt must be called. The hurting and counter-hurting has to stop. So, why *start*?

The anger was one thing. The anger at being followed by the private detective character, and the reason for him being there. The anger at the poison-pen letter. The anger at Evans for sending that letter. That anger (those angers). They were justified. But the tongue-lashing I gave Maude had little to do with those angers. It stemmed from something far deeper and far longer. From years of tiny hurts she'd inflicted on me. A sort of vengeance. But, if so, a very petty and very disgraceful vengeance. She was Maude. Allowances had to be made. The truth? What I think is the truth? I'd made too many 'allowances'. I was tired, dog-weary, of making allowances. I was, I suppose, 'catching up'. Evening things out a little.

Remember the film *Love Story*? We saw it together years ago. The four of us. Remember that famous line? 'Love means never having to say you're sorry.' A wonderful line, Harry. If only such perfection was possible!

Maude has never said 'Sorry'. Not once that I can remember. But that's not the same thing, is it? Never *having* to say 'Sorry' means never deliberately hurting. Never having the *need* to say 'Sorry'.

Last night I could have said 'Sorry'. I could have dropped to my knees and begged forgiveness. One part of me wanted to, but another part (the part which knows Maude so well) realised the hopelessness of doing so. It would have been tantamount to handing the whip back to her . . . and she'd have used it. Oh, my God! Hurt or *be* hurt. What a choice to be left with. What a way to live a life.

I saw the tears come. Real tears. Not the mock-tears of a spoiled child. I went to bed. She followed some time later. I slept badly, if at all. I could hear her sobbing in the other bed. I wanted to go across and comfort her, but couldn't bring myself to do so.

Today (all today and even to the time I came here, into the study, to make this entry) we've played the stupid game of 'armed neutrality'. A conversation limited to please-pass-the-salt remarks. Great chunks of polite silence. Strangers, who just happen to be married to each other. On the face of it not particularly *liking* each other.

46

You remember those periods? When you were a teenager you opted out. Remember? You retired to your own room, and let us get on with it. You didn't understand. God grant you never *will* understand. That you and Ben never lose the ability to *communicate*. Row? Of course you'll row. You love each other far too much not to row occasionally. You'll row, you'll call each other names, you'll say things you don't mean, then one of you will see the stupidity of it and laugh aloud, then the other will join in the laughter, and you'll kiss and make-up. That's being married, Harry. That's the very core of a happy marriage. The marriage begins to turn sour when the laughter doesn't come. When there's no kissing and no making up. When (like us) the anger and the hurt merely fades, leaving a vacuum. A polite, good-mannered nothing. There's nothing to build on. There's no foundation for a fresh start. Just the knowledge that it's going to happen again. One more flare-up, followed by a fading away, followed by another flare-up. Until one of us dies. Not a happy prospect. Not a happy future.

In God's name, don't let it happen to you!

The letter from Evans? I suppose I could have shown it to our local constable, P.C. Pinter. I had it in mind, but thought better of it. I think a court case, with all the washing of dirty linen (even though it *isn't* dirty) is what Evans wants. I think that's why he did nothing to disguise his handwriting. A fine, perhaps. Nothing more drastic and, at a guess, not too big a fine at that. As far as he's concerned it would be worth it for the bad publicity as far as the firm's concerned.

He's an evil man. I wish I'd taken your advice and called the police when we found him to be a thief.

THURSDAY, 2ND DECEMBER

I have a good son. A fine son. A very wise son. That he will, eventually, read these words does not alter their truth. Thank you, Harry, for pointing out the obvious to a fool of a father. For making the suggestion you made this morning.

'How long since you had a holiday, pa?'

That was the question, and I couldn't answer it. Ten years? Twelve years? I could not answer it with certainty. I love my work. I don't *need* holidays. I explained that, too. And with both conviction and honesty.

'And what about ma?'

Something else I hadn't thought of. That Maude *hadn't* a firm to build up. That her life wasn't as full as mine. That, because she isn't the gregarious type, she might be lonely. Undoubtedly *is* lonely, for long stretches at a time. Bored, too. Our marriage. Wrecking itself on the rocks of boredom. A possibility and more than a possibility. My fault. Selfishness, on my part.

An architecturally-designed house, tucked away on the outskirts of a nice little village. Nothing skimped. Beautifully decorated. Magnificent views. More than an acre of well-kept gardens. Every labour-saving device on the market. You name it, it's all there. But if it's all there, plus boredom . . . then what?

Maybe that's what's been wrong with Maude all these years.

'Before Christmas,' suggested Harry.

'I couldn't. I . . .'

'You *could*. Come on, pa. A nice quiet break, before the festivities start. It's what you need. What you deserve.'

What *I* need? Or what *Maude* needs?

It was a good idea Harry. A real life-saver . . . or should I say marriage-saver?

She's not been too bad these last two weeks. A little touchy, but as long as I gave a little thought before I said anything she's even smiled occasionally. And when *she's* been snappy I've deliberately let it pass.

This evening, when I told her, her eyes lit up. End of all argument. End of all hesitation.

I think on principle more than anything, she said, 'It's the wrong time of year for holidaying.'

'A good hotel.'

'It can be cold. And damp.'

'A good hotel,' I repeated. 'Central heating as good as ours. We can warn them. The beds to be warm and aired. Any hint of

48

dampness, and we won't stay. And when we go out, we have the clothes. Fur coats. Lined jackets and boots. Who cares? Just a change of environment. We both need it.'

'It sounds nice. If it can be arranged.'

'Tomorrow.' I made the snap decision, while she was in the mood. 'I'll telephone now. Make it a long weekend. Tomorrow until Tuesday morning. Then, I'll ring Harry and break the news.'

'Where?' She was almost breathless. God, she was *excited* about something at last. I'd broken through.

I checked *Egon Ronay*. Very carefully. For the first time in months (months or years?) Maude was on what I imagine modern parlance might call 'a high'.

'I'll – I'll go upstairs. Start packing.'

'Fine. Fine.' I thumbed the pages of *Egon Ronay*. 'Just leave everything to me. The coast?' I asked.

'We *live* in the country.'

'Right. The coast it is.'

'I'll go and pack.'

I tried four hotels before I was satisfied. The first two had bored-sounding receptionists. *They* were doing *me* a favour! Dammit, at high season, with every bed taken, they couldn't have shown less interest. The third sounded okay, but they had the painters in.

'They won't be in the way, sir.'

'There'll be the smell of paint.'

'A little, perhaps. But it won't spoil your holiday. We – er – we have to re-decorate when we can.'

' "A little" is too much. I'm sorry.'

'I'm sorry too, sir. Some other time, perhaps?'

'Some other time,' I promised.

The fourth seemed to be the one I was after.

'Twin beds or double sir?'

On an impulse I said, 'Double.' Then I asked, 'An electric blanket . . . to make sure it's warm?'

'That can be arranged, sir. The sheets. Linen? Nylon? If you wish, flannelette.'

'Flannelette.' It seemed a good, old-fashioned idea. I said, 'What about the central heating?'

49

'You can regulate the heat from your own room, sir. Two radiators. As warm as you're likely to want it, sir.'

'The view?'

'Over the fields to the cliff-edge, sir. Then the sea. They're all double-glazed, but they'll open easily enough if you want sea air.'

'It sounds the sort of place I'm after,' I admitted.

'Thank you, sir. Any complaints, however trivial, let them know at the reception desk. It will be seen to immediately. You said tomorrow, sir?'

'Tomorrow,' I verified. 'Until Tuesday.'

'About what time tomorrow?'

'Lunch time. Thereabouts.'

'Lunch ends at two o'clock, sir.' Then, hurriedly, 'But you can order late lunch, now. We'll keep the chef on duty until you arrive.'

'What choice?' I asked.

'I'd suggest Dover sole, sir. I can recommend it.'

'Fresh?'

'Sir.' There was a quiet, polite chuckle over the wire. 'At this moment, it's still swimming around in the North Sea.'

'Dover sole it is.' I returned the chuckle. 'With trimmings. We'll try to be there before two.'

'Don't worry, sir. *We'll* do the worrying. *You're* on holiday.'

Now *that*, Harry my son, is the way a good hotel gets custom and keeps custom. To make the customer happy before he even *sees* the place. Priorities. Like we run the firm. The customer counts. Whilever he signs the cheque (and as long as the cheque doesn't bounce) *he* says what he wants . . . and, if at all possible, he gets it. I don't give too much of a damn about sunshine. Browning yourself, like toast under a grill, is *not* my idea of getting value for money. I want pampering. I want Maude to be pampered. *That's* being on holiday.

And now, for bed. Maude has already packed a couple of suitcases. Draped coats on hangers to hang in the back of the car. I still have my own things to get ready. Then, the sheets.

Flannelette sheets should be very nice. God, the very thought brings back memories.

Thanks, Harry. Thanks for making the suggestion. When I get back to this diary thing, I'll let you know how we enjoyed ourselves.

To do something with my hands. To do something with my brain. To do *something*!

A record is necessary. For you, Harry. In order that, at some future date, you may read and (perhaps) understand. The trivia, as well as the important things. The trivia, too, is important. Indeed, nothing is *un*important. To understand. To understand *everything*, including my own feelings and emotions.

I must control myself. Try to. Force myself to remember each moment. Refuse (in effect) to go mad. For your sake. A cold-blooded, detailed record of *exactly* what happened.

The hotel was all we could have wished for. Faultless service. A standard of cleanliness beyond reproach. Fine food, magnificently prepared and presented. Even Maude was impressed.

The room, too. A beautiful room. Spacious, warm and with a wonderful view out to the sea's horizon. The double bed? I watched Maude's face as she entered the room and saw the bed for the first time. Nothing! Neither approval nor disapproval. As if we'd never *not* slept together. A simple, normal acceptance of what, on the face of things, we were used to.

At lunch (we arrived in good time for lunch) we met our fellow-guests. A man called Foster and his wife. Just the four of us. Foster (he seemed to go out of his way to impart the information) was a master at a comprehensive school. He'd suffered a nervous breakdown. He'd also won a football pool prize. Hence their presence at a hotel which was obviously well beyond their normal means. He sported a drooping moustache and long hair. He wore heavy boots (even in the dining room!) baggy flannels, a none-too-clean turtle-necked sweater and God only knows how many pins and badges in the lapels of an ancient tweed jacket. His wife was the sort of woman that type of man marries. Their names were Raymond and Martha . . . and I wasn't surprised! *Snob!*

They were vegetarians and anti-just-about-everything. Part of

51

the 'back to nature' crowd. A normal conversation with them was out of the question. They didn't know it (they hadn't the sense to realise it) but they were the laughing-stock of the hotel staff.

We'd hardly sat down at the table before he clomped across the dining room, held out a hand as big as a ham, and said, 'Foster. I think we're fellow-guests.'

'Really?'

'Raymond Foster. That's my wife, over there. Martha.'

I looked across and (I swear!) she raised a hand in a coy wave.

'Physics master, at a comprehensive. A spot too much over-work. Cracked up. Better now, though. Won a small packet on the pools, so decided to have an out-of-season break. Two weeks, bird-watching.'

I saw the look of annoyance on Maude's face.

'We're about to eat,' I said.

'Ah! We've just finished.'

'You'll be leaving, then?'

'What?'

'The dining room. I'm sure there must be thousands of birds, waiting to be watched.'

'Ah, yes. Yes, of course.' The damn fool thought I'd made a joke and guffawed loudly. He withdrew the hand I hadn't bothered to shake, and said, 'See you at dinner then.'

He lumbered towards the door, his wife joined him and they left.

The meal was delicious and, because she'd left her bed earlier than usual, Maude decided to have a quiet afternoon snooze. I settled myself in a comfortable chair in the lounge, filled and lighted my pipe, ordered coffee and, between glancing through the pages of a decent selection of magazines, watched the rain pour down beyond the double-glazed window. The wicked thought struck me that the only birds likely to be available for the Fosters to watch would be ducks.

They were soon back. At least, *he* was . . . I presumed his wife had gone up to their room. He thumped across the carpet and flopped into the armchair next to mine.

'It's peeing down out there,' he said.

I didn't answer.

He picked up one of the magazines and brazenly wafted the

52

smoke from my pipe away from his face.

'You're killing yourself,' he proclaimed solemnly.

'Really?'

'The muck you're dragging into your lungs. Ever seen the lungs of a smoker?'

'A pleasure I've so far denied myself.'

'Full of goo. A filthy habit.'

I ignored him. He was an idiot, and I treated him as such. He refused to be ignored.

He said, 'You'll be a flesh-eater, too?'

Somehow, he gave the impression of a Solomon making wise, throw-away remarks about some half-wit incapable of understanding what was being said. And, all the time, he kept using the magazine as a makeshift fan.

I stared at the lunatic. Never before had I come across such crass ill-manners.

'Dead meat,' he amplified. 'Like most people. Martha and I have more sense.'

I lost all patience with the young pup. I fear I became very rude. Very basic.

'You don't smoke?' I said gently.

'No. We've more sense. We . . .'

'You don't eat meat?'

'I've already said. We . . .'

'You're married, are you?'

'Of course.' He stared. 'We're not . . .'

'Have you got round to screwing each other yet? Or is *that* bad for your health?' Then, while he was still gaping, I tapped one of the badges on his lapel with the stem of my pipe. 'C.N.D?'

'If it's any of your . . .'

'I'm making it my business, sonny. You're shoving your nose into my life, I'm shoving my nose into yours. C.N.D. And you're a physics master. How do you make the two tally? Without nuclear physics there'd be no bomb. All I'm doing is killing myself . . . *if* I'm doing that. What you flash boys are doing – have already done – is dealing in megadeath. Other people.' I allowed it time to sink in, then snapped, 'Now, get from under my feet, little man. And take your wife with you. Go watch your birds. Maybe they don't think you're a damn nuisance.'

And now, having told you all this, I wonder why. Compared with other things my run-in with an unimportant crank is of no importance. Other, that is, than that I wanted Maude to be happy. I didn't want anything, or anybody, to spoil her holiday. And she didn't like the Fosters. I'd already seen the tiny signs. She didn't like them therefore they *were* capable of ruining everything.

You know your mother, Harry. Little things tend to be magnified. They become big things. Things upon which to hang disproportionate complaints. I have to be careful. We all have to be careful. It's part of our life. Always has been. To tread very carefully, in case we upset Maude.

I'm not complaining. My fault, I suppose, for being weaker than I should have been. Normality (the normality of the ups and downs of ordinary life) is something she hasn't learned to cope with. Hasn't *had* to cope with. I've gone out of my way to shelter her from them, and there's a price to pay.

But in this case even that isn't quite true. Quite fair. *I* didn't like the Fosters either. They represent (represented) something beyond my understanding. The you're-a-fool-we-can-do-things-much-better crowd. The placard-wavers. The marchers and the demonstrators. The lunatic fringe incapable of holding beliefs without ramming those beliefs down everybody's throat. The nuisance-makers who *refuse* to be told to go away.

Therefore, I'd let fly at Foster. Deliberately insulted him. It was the only way. Short of an out-and-out insult he (and his precious wife, no doubt) would have imposed themselves and their lunatic beliefs upon us . . . and that would have been the end of Maude's happiness.

The dinner made up for everything.

(The Fosters weren't there. One must presume they'd found some nuts-and-lettuce establishment farther along the coast!)

Nevertheless, the dining room was more than half-filled. Locals, and people who'd come from miles around. Friday evening, you see. The end of the working week and, if you were prepared to pay

54

the price, an excellent meal (a truly excellent choice of dishes) and a pleasant celebration of the close of one more slice of the rat-race and, at the same time, two days of relaxation.

The Fosters would have been well out of their depth. (Perhaps one reason why they weren't there.) I suspect the blanket description of the diners and their wives (one must give them the benefit of any doubt, and assume they were their wives) is covered by the expression 'professional men'. Doctors, solicitors, accountants, bank managers and the like. Quite a few wore dinner jackets and black bow-ties. Most of the ladies (including Maude) wore ankle-length dresses. There was class there, and Maude seemed to hug it around her, like an invisible stole, and she was happier than I'd seen her for years.

The diners all seemed to know each other (one must assume that they all dined there fairly regularly) and they allowed us into their company without hesitation. The easy laughter. The 'in' jokes we didn't really appreciate. The drinking of a little more wine than we had planned.

After the meal everybody seemed to gravitate to the bar lounge where the same joviality was continued. Maude laughed. I forget what the remark was, but it was made by a youngish chap who, with his wife, shared our table, and Maude laughed. Aloud, and for some considerable time. Harry you know Maude. You know, as well as I do, that one of her many yardsticks via which she always assessed whether or not a person was what she called 'common' was laughing aloud. But *she* laughed aloud.

It was like a break-through. Like winning a great prize. As stunning and as wonderful as that. That prolonged burst of spontaneous laughter. I remember thinking . . . No – probably not thinking – *hoping*. Perhaps even praying . . .

Before your time, Harry. Before you were born, and when you were too young to remember. You may, perhaps, remember odd moments, but not the *real* Maude. The Maude I paid court to. The Maude who stood with me at the altar rail. A great person, Harry. A gloriously happy person. Nobody marries a shrew. I certainly didn't. I married the most perfect woman I'd ever met. We had the world. We had *everything*.

What in God's name happens to people after they've been

55

married for some years? What happens? Why does it happen? How does it happen and when does it happen?

(The truth, Harry. The truth, because if I don't tell the truth at this moment, it never *will* be told. The small hours have a very cleansing effect upon the mind. After the tiredness there comes a purity of thought. A discarding of pretence. Like now. Like this very moment.)

Harry, Harry, Harry . . . what *happens* to people? How can two people, so much in love, so content merely to be in each other's company, drift so far apart? We change. Of course we change, but that's no *reason*. Age of itself is no answer. Change comes with age (agreed) but must it be change for the worse? Must the years turn love into eternal bickering? Must time sour what was once so sweet?

And if it does, if it must, does it *always* happen? Is *every* marriage like ours? A facade of mock-respectability? A play-acting for everybody other than the man and wife? It can't be always – not *always*! – otherwise the world would be mad.

Who knows? Maybe it is.

Forgive me. I digressed, unashamedly. I intend to tell what happened, and end up seeking an impossible truth and asking unanswerable questions. I have had coffee. Black and strong. I have smoked a pipe of tobacco. At a guess, were I to open the blinds of my study I might see the first signs of dawn. No matter. I am not tired, and the story must be recorded while memory is fresh.

The Friday evening. The Friday she laughed aloud. She was happy. We were both happy and, I think, a little drunk. It was almost midnight when the party (it had developed into a spontaneous party) . . . when the party broke up, the others went to their cars and Maude and I took the lift to our room.

The double bed. Remember? As we entered the room, it didn't mock me. It invited me. Maude, too, or so I thought. She made no comment. Indeed, as she undressed prior to soaking in the bath, she smiled. Even chuckled quietly to herself. A different Maude. A Maude like the old Maude. God, I was happy.

I flopped into the armchair, waited until she'd finished with the bathroom then I, too, soaked a little tiredness from my body in the hot, sudsed water. I felt younger. Younger than I'd felt in years. I needed the break. Maude, too. Both of us. I was sure of that. To laugh a little more. We'd made it. The fight was over. The firm was as solid as a rock, and I had a son ready to fill my shoes the minute I decided to retire. We had a lovely home, in a beautiful part of the country. We had years of life ahead of us. Good years. Years in which we could catch up on what it had needed to get us to where we were. We could afford things. We could damn near afford *anything*. So, where was the problem? Let's forget our middle age. Let's pretend to be a little younger. No great pretence. We were both healthy. Neither of us had worries worth a damn. Why not try to recapture some of that love we'd once had for each other?

Great God!

Mortification can be a terrible thing. To be made to feel foul, for no reason at all. To be made to feel unclean. An animal. A woman can do that to you, Harry. A woman can take what little manhood you have left and make you feel dirty. Bestial. All this by doing nothing. What is it they say? That ancient joke? 'Stare at the ceiling and think of England.' Good God, I wasn't trying to produce another monarch. I was trying to show love. A form of love. A gentle, but passionate love we seemed to have lost. A love she wanted no part of. A love which disgusted her, and she did nothing to hide her disgust. She turned her face as I tried to kiss her.

'No. Not on the lips. It's unhygenic.'

Unhygenic!

Had I been diseased she could have shown no more repugnance.

It wasn't even a farce. It was something which could have been beautiful (something I *wanted* to be beautiful) turned inside-out and made ugly.

The details? The details are unimportant. Just that my world crashed, every last hope vanished and I turned my back on her and silently wept. When we got home I'd move out of her bedroom. Permanently. No more. No more humiliation. No more pretence. The marriage was finished. We'd live under the same roof. *Her* life wouldn't alter (I owed her that for the once-upon-a-time) and, to

outward appearances we'd still be the same 'John and Maude'.
But privately in our own secret little world . . . *nothing*.

A little like dying. Oh, yes. No exaggeration. Something deep
down inside dies. It doesn't merely sleep. Lies dormant. Remains
undisturbed for days, or weeks, or months. Not even for years. It
dies. And you know. You can't kid yourself any more. It's gone
forever. It's *dead*!

And you feel the loss. My God, how you feel the loss.

On the Saturday (Saturday, December 4th) I was up and out
before Maude awakened. I walked along lanes, between hedges.
Don't ask me where. Just walking. Savouring the clean air from the
sea. Lonely. Above all else, lonely. Odd . . . I didn't feel the cold.
Perhaps because I was too cold inside. I noticed paper-thin ice still
covering the puddles and ruck-marks in the mud leading to field
gates. It must have rained heavily during the night. There must
have been a moderate ground frost. Indeed it must have still been
cold, but the temperature had no effect upon me.

Maude had already started her breakfast when I got back. I
caught a glimpse of the Fosters, presumably setting out for a bird-
watching expedition, as I entered the dining room, and the
thought flashed through my mind . . .

A passing thought, you understand. A nothing. Some tiny
stupidity triggered off by my own misery. Foster was an ill-
mannered lout. His wife was as big a crank as he was. *But they were
holding hands.* They had nothing . . . yet they had far more than we
had. All *we* had was comparative wealth.

Maude was distantly polite. The same old technique she'd
honed to such a cutting edge.

'Couldn't you sleep?'

'Not too well, dear.' And (I admit it) my conversational coinage
matched hers. 'I drank a little too much last night.'

'Was *that* it?'

'I think it must have been.'

'You must drink less in future.'

'Quite.'

What an insane conversation between a man and his wife. What
bitingly bitter insults wrapped up in that exchange. And yet (I

swear) one part of me wanted me to drop to my knees, damn the waiters, and plead, 'Why? *Why*? WHY?'

We finished the meal in silence, then one of us (it might have been me, but I'm not sure) suggested a stroll. Along the cliffs. Some sea air. Anything. Anything to kill time before lunch.

That's how it happened. Just a stroll along the top of the cliffs. No notices warning of danger. Just a well-worn, muddy path through the grass and the jagged edge of the cliff. And the tide was full and pounding the base of the cliffs. And there was this V which seemed to have been bitten out of the cliff. Dangerous? I suppose so. But not in dry weather. Only dangerous when the path was wet and slippery with mud. And she was walking in front of me. Less than a yard in front of me. And I saw the slip of one of her feet. That first slip which threw her off balance and made her throw up her arms to steady herself, but she couldn't before the other foot slipped.

Then she toppled. Head first. And the scream was caught in the wind and meant nothing.

How long did I stand there on the edge of the cliff looking down at her? What were my feelings?

She was dead. She *had* to be dead. The V was no width at all, and she must have struck projections on the way down. She was lying, broken-backed, between two boulders and for most of the time the dirty-grey foam splashed and swirled across her face. Into her open mouth. Across her face. The filth and muck which had collected in the wash and swirl of the tide clinging to her clothes. I knew damn well she was dead, but for the first few moments it meant nothing.

Feeling returned. My mind started functioning again.

I tried to be horrified. I honestly *tried* to be horrified. But it was no good. Not at first. God help me, the first real feeling I had was one of relief. A wicked feeling. A shameful feeling. But it was there.

Not (and please believe this, Harry) not relief that I was 'free'. A far more complex relief than that. *She* was 'free'. I think some part of the relief stemmed from that realisation. The end of her unhappy life suddenly, unexpectedly and with a minimum of fear and (hopefully) a minimum of pain. In the last few years (probably more than a few) her life must have been hell. A mental hell. A hell,

59

in the main, of her own making, but no less of a hell for that. And perhaps not *all* of her own making. The possibility entered my head for the first time. That broken thing at the base of the cliff. *My* fault? At least *part* my fault? What sort of a husband had I been? Not *my* assessment. *Her* assessment. And if I'd gone wrong why hadn't she told me? Or *had* she told me? In her own way. Told me (hinted, perhaps) but had I been too deaf, too blind, to notice the hints? Had *I* made her what she'd become?

Harry, time means nothing to the mind. Thoughts, recriminations, might-have-beens, flash past while time stands still. They were all there, but for the moment the foremost was that of a kind of relief. For her . . . and for myself.

I didn't want rid of her. As God's my judge, I didn't want rid of her. I didn't want her dead. I didn't want her 'out of the way'. I certainly didn't want another woman. Anybody else. So what *did* I want? What was the basis for this strange feeling of relief?

Selfishness, I suppose. A few years of peace. The rest of my life, what was left of it, without the ever-present gnawing worry that 'Maude might not like it'. But, given the choice, I'd have accepted that, I'd have accepted *anything*, for her still to be alive.

Anything!

The mood changed. I suddenly felt what I *should* have felt. The one-time-adoration came back like a tidal wave, and for a moment I almost threw myself down on top of her. She was broken. She was shattered. The only woman I'd ever loved . . . she didn't exist any more.

I can't really remember my run back to the hotel. I think the mind closes a door at a certain point. I know the manager telephoned the police, the cliff-rescue people, then you and that, when you and Ben arrived, I almost broke. The nearest thing I've yet been to tears. The identification. The Inquest. 'Death by Misadventure'. The so-called 'arrangements'. And then this afternoon . . . strictly speaking *yesterday* afternoon, because a new morning has arrived since I started this entry.

There was a finality as the coffin slid between the curtains. It was far more than 'The End'. It was the closing of the book. Ben wept. You, too, I think. I wept inside, but the tears wouldn't come.

So many times in the past. So much heartbreak fastened tight and not being allowed freedom to show itself. One day, God willing, I'll be able to unwind. Even sleep without the fear of nightmares. One day. Some day.

Eventually, I think I'll put this house up for sale. The house and the contents. Everything! Too many memories, both good and bad. Perhaps that's what 'haunting' boils down to. Because she's still here. Upstairs in the main bedroom. It needs a deliberate effort of will to force the realisation through that wall. That she *isn't*. That she ended, ceased to be, at the bottom of a cliff with the soiled surf splashing and boiling across her face and over her smashed body.

That she just *isn't* any more!

I love you, Harry. That, too, needs recording. That, as son, friend and business partner, you couldn't be bettered. That, bad though these last few days have been, they'd have been infinitely worse without you and Ben.

And now, sleep of a sort. A hot drink. Some whisky. An armchair, perhaps. Something approximating sleep, and the hope that this pain (this madness) might ease a little. That this strange, unwarranted feeling of sadness mixed with guilt isn't with me forever.

PART TWO

The Accusation of Raymond Foster

The local authority had again tried to make ends meet. As always, they weren't too flush. As always, until they were mugged or burgled, the rate-payers tended to figure coppers as something of a luxury. So, as always, the local authority had done what they'd done for the last ten years; they'd postponed the building of a new sub-divisional police headquarters to some future and, as yet, not-agreed-upon date. A lick of paint, a couple of hardboard partition walls to make two rooms where there'd previously been one: that until they started the same old round of arguments next year.

Meanwhile, the fuzz-house was nice and warm. Small rooms may be cramped, but they're cosy. One wall-heater and something not much bigger than a dog kennel soon warms up. Sure, the files were stacked upon files, and those files were stacked upon *other* files but, looking on the bright side, paper is a damn good insulator and, although they could rarely find the sheet they were looking for, the one thing they had in abundance was paper. Paper, filing cabinets, desks, tables, chairs, book-cases – more office equipment than *that* – and, if the cops had to move crab-fashion to reach point B from point A, who cared? They shouldn't be *in* the sub-divisional headquarters. Their place was out on the streets, where all the action took place.

Some action!

'The thing about bobbying,' said the uniformed sergeant gravely, 'is this. Take it a day at a time. One day more, one day less. By the book. None of this "top of the head" stuff. By the book, and you can't be faulted.'

'Yes, sergeant.'

The young constable wasn't really listening. He'd heard it all before. At least a dozen times with minor variations. This particular three-striper liked the sound of his own voice; loved to impart un-asked-for wisdom; had it all stitched up and tied in pink ribbon and wanted everybody to be aware of that fact.

'Take superintendents . . .'

The constable's silent prayer was answered. Some unseen customer had thumbed the bell-push and the ring interrupted the sergeant in mid-sentence. The sergeant frowned mild annoyance. The constable almost jumped to his feet, dodged around the furniture and made for what was laughingly called the 'Public Counter'.

The constable knew that some police stations really *did* have counters. Even section stations. He'd seen them. As big as bar-counters, some of them. Polished and shiny, and sometimes even with a telephone. He wished the one at the sub-divisional headquarters was like that, or at least a little less like the glass-fronted box-office at a back-street cinema. He wished it wasn't necessary to bend the head sideways in order to exchange conversation through the concaved-top opening. He wished . . .

More than anything, he wished something would *happen*.

He bent down a little, felt the usual berk, and said, 'Yes, sir.'

'My name's – er . . .' The man touched one end of his moustache nervously. 'My name's Foster. I wish to report a murder.'

'A mu . . .' The constable's mouth slackened, before he could complete the word.

'A murder,' said Foster a little more firmly. 'I've seen a man push his wife over the cliff.'

'J-just now?'

'No. Three days ago.'

'Three days . . .' The constable held up a hand, as if stopping traffic, then gabbled, 'Look, don't go away, sir. Don't go away. I'll – er – I'll get somebody with . . .' As he hurried back to the sergeant, he almost pleaded, 'Don't go away, sir.'

They'd moved Eastlight box files from one of the spare chairs, and Foster was repeating his story to the uniformed sergeant.

Foster felt hemmed-in. Trapped. Almost panic-stricken. He'd never been inside a police station before and he'd never imagined it

66

to be like *this*. Despite the white paint, dingy. Like a trap, with its jaws already half-closed.

'Three days ago?' mused the sergeant.

'Yes.'

'That would be Saturday. The day the Duxbury woman fell over the edge.'

'She didn't "fall". She was pushed,' breathed Foster desperately.

The sergeant nodded slowly. Ponderously.

'We've sent for the C.I.D,' he said. 'Their side of things, see?'

'Can't *you* . . .'

'I could, but they wouldn't like it,' said the sergeant.

'I – I don't see why . . .'

'The right way, the wrong way, son. What are you? Schoolteacher?'

'Physics master.'

'You should know, then. Start as you mean to go on.'

'Look, I came here . . .'

'You took your time,' said the sergeant, with mild censure.

'It's – it's not the sort of thing . . .'

'Death by Misadventure. That's what the Coroner's Court found.'

'It *wasn't*. It was . . .'

'For the moment that's the verdict, see? Recorded. Over. Finished with. Coroners are important people.'

'I – I wish . . .'

'They don't like their verdicts messed about with.'

'I wish I hadn't come.' Foster moved his hands along the thighs of his trousers to rid the palms of sweat. 'Couldn't we . . .'

'What?'

'Forget it.' It was little more than a whispered moan. 'Y'know, forget I called in. I – er – I don't *know* the Duxburys. It's – it's nothing to me. Not *really*. It's just that . . .'

'Nothing to you that a woman might have been murdered?'

The sergeant looked outraged. It wasn't bad acting for an on-the-spot effort. He'd have *loved* to have forgotten it, but the book of words didn't cater for contrived 'forgetfulness'. Therefore he continued to mark time, pending the arrival of Detective Sergeant Harker, at which point (and with luck) he *could* 'forget it'.

another Harry?

Harry Harker could straighten up a Rubic Cube in thirty minutes flat. He couldn't do *The Times* crossword puzzle within soft-boiled-egg time, but given a couple of hours every square would be accurately lettered, and without the aid of reference books or dictionaries. This didn't make him a genius, of course, but it gave a clue to the sort of mind he possessed. It held things. It remembered. North of the brow-line a million little pigeon-holes held carefully docketed snippets of information. Names, addresses, telephone numbers, dates, car registration numbers, descriptions, CRO numbers, news items going back thirty years and more. Anything. Everything. If he read something, saw something or heard something . . . it just stayed. Nothing deliberate. Nothing he'd practised. Just a quirk of mind he'd been born with.

good

It was one reason why he was a damn good detective.

Another reason was that he didn't *look* like a detective. He limped a little, having smashed almost every bone in his left foot in a car accident. Because he limped, he was never without a walking-stick; a walking-stick of well-seasoned hickory which, every week without fail, he rubbed down with linseed oil. To complete the picture, he favoured heavy Harris tweed. Winter or summer. A Harris tweed suit, complete with waistcoat, sporting gold watch-chain and a half-hunter in its upper left-hand pocket. He was also beginning to spread out a little. Middle age and not enough exercise. But that was okay with Harry Harker. The more you hurried, the quicker you reached that final hole in Mother Earth.

He switched off the engine, opened the door of the Fiesta, hoisted himself from the driving seat, reached back in for the walking stick, then slammed the door. Foster closed the nearside door and followed Harker to the cliff edge.

'This is where it happened,' said Harker.

'Yes . . . about here.'

'*Right* here.' Harker didn't deal with 'abouts'. He pointed with the stick. 'That bite out of the edge. That's where she went over. Accidentally or with help. Now where were you?'

'Over there.' Foster raised an arm. 'That knoll. Behind that line of bushes.'

'A hundred yards. Thereabouts.'

'About that.'

Harker began to walk towards the small rise. Foster fell in step.

'You had the binoculars on them,' said Harker.

'We were watching the gulls, actually. We thought we'd seen a kittiwake.'

'Black-headed,' grunted Harker.

'What?'

'No kittiwakes along this stretch of the coast. Black-headed gulls. They shed the dark facial feathers in winter. They're not as obvious.'

Foster didn't like being contradicted.

He said, 'I had the binoculars on him.'

'What make?' asked Harker.

'Eh?'

'The binoculars?'

'Oh – er – Yashica.'

'Magnification?'

'Eight by forty.'

'Not bad.' Harker slowed a little as they began to mount the rise. 'But morning. You'd be looking into the sun. Reflection from the sea wouldn't help.'

'They have coated lenses.'

They walked in silence until they reached the line of bushes.

'Right . . . where?' asked Harker.

Foster hesitated a moment, then walked a few steps and said, 'Here. With Martha on my left.'

'Kneeling down? Squatting?' Harker joined him.

'Lying full-length. On our stomachs. Elbows resting on the ground.'

'Watching this gull?'

'Yes.'

'Both of you?'

'Yes.'

'Both with binoculars?'

'No. We've just the one pair. We shared them.'

69

Question followed question. Gruffly but quietly asked. Short and to the point, like tiny brush-strokes which would eventually build up a complete picture. Yes, they'd both seen the Duxburys walking along the cliff path. No, they hadn't appeared to be quarrelling. They'd been walking, Indian-file-fashion – Duxbury behind his wife. No, he was quite sure the Duxburys hadn't seen them. Yes, he'd been watching the gull in flight, and the swing of the binoculars had suddenly included the Duxburys, just as he'd pushed her over the edge of the cliff. Yes, he'd seen her topple before she disappeared. No, he hadn't seen the actual physical contact, as Duxbury pushed, but Duxbury's hands and arms had still been extended, immediately after he *had* pushed her. No, there was no doubt at all. Not an atom of doubt.

'Fine, he pushed her.' Harker rested both hands on the crook of his walking-stick and gazed out to sea. 'For the sake of argument, let's say he pushed her . . .'

'He did. I'm sure he did.'

'Then what?'

'He stood looking down at her.'

'Why?'

'I – I don't know.'

'You'd have lost interest in the gull by this time.'

'Of course.'

'Binoculars on Duxbury.'

'Yes.'

'Some sort of expression on his face, surely?'

'He – he was half-turned. It's difficult.'

'Satisfaction?'

'No.' Foster spoke carefully. 'That wasn't the impression.'

'A job well done?'

'No.' Foster shook his head, hesitated, then said, 'If anything, shock.'

'Or waiting to see if she was dead?'

'That, too, I suppose.'

'How long did he stay there?'

'Ten minutes.' Foster sighed. 'At least ten minutes. We thought he'd never go.'

'Just looking at her?'

70

Foster nodded.

'You didn't make yourself known?'

'Good Lord, no.' Foster sounded almost shocked at the question.

'Why?'

'Good God, if he'd just killed his wife . . .'

'*If?*' Harker snapped at the word, like a terrier pouncing on a rat.

'Well, he *had*.'

'So, why qualify it?'

'I'm not. It was a figure of speech.'

'Room for possible doubt,' grunted Harker.

'No. No doubt at all.'

Harker straightened, and said, 'We'll go back to the hotel.'

'The . . .'

'See your wife.'

'I'd rather . . .' Foster had to quicken his step to catch up with Harker. 'I'd rather she wasn't brought into this thing.'

'Why?'

'She abhors violence.'

'I'm not going to hit her.'

'No. I didn't mean . . .'

'At the moment,' said Harker, 'and even assuming you're telling the truth, it's two against one. You say she was pushed. Duxbury says she fell. And Duxbury's version wins, hands down, thanks to a little thing called the Presumption of Innocence.'

'Is it *really* necessary . . .'

'Yes, it's *really* necessary. That and a few more things.'

Fate often treats what few innocents there are left in the world very kindly. Take Martha Foster. A little girl, complete with passionate beliefs, encased in the body of a fully grown, if slight, woman. Not for her the militant screams for Equal Rights. She was a wife; a mere woman; a happy and willing slave to the man who'd taken her under his wing. What *he* thought, *she* thought . . . obviously. To have openly disagreed would have been tantamount to mutiny. He'd promised to look after her for the rest of her life, and that deserved gratitude far and beyond anything she could ever hope to show. Ah well, kismet had taken a hand and pushed her into the arms of Raymond Foster, so she just *might* get away with not being hurt too badly.

She wore a kaftan, tied at the waist with a sash. The sleeves reached to the tips of her fingers, and little more than three inches of jeans, then her bare feet, peeped from beneath its lower edge. She sat on the edge of the bed and, periodically, jerked her head to keep the shoulder-length hair from her face.

'Raymond's told you,' she said in a sad little voice.

Harker nodded. He lowered himself into a cane armchair and waited. This child/woman had to be treated gently. Her world was as thin and brittle as a Christmas tree bauble, and it would have been wicked to heel it into tiny fragments without cause.

Harker waited.

'He shouldn't have done,' she said solemnly. 'He's been ill.'

'He won't be hurt,' promised Harker gently.

'You don't know. You . . .'

'Darling, we can't watch murder committed and not say anything.'

'He's right,' smiled Harker.

'He hasn't slept since it happened. And he's been *ill*.'

'Did you see it?' asked Harker.

'Not really.' She raised a hand to push the hair from her face. 'I need spectacles to read with, and my distant vision isn't very good.'

'What *did* you see?' asked Harker, quietly.

'I saw them walking along the path.'

'Recognise them?'

'Yes, I suppose so. Raymond said . . .'

'Ah, but did *you* recognise them?'

'I think so.' The answer was a little unsure. 'Not what they were wearing, but the way they walked. Mrs Duxbury, very stiff and upright. He was bent forward a little. Round shouldered.'

'Nobody else about?'

'No. Just Raymond and me . . . and the Duxburys.'

'Raymond and *I*, Martha darling.'

'I'm sorry. Raymond and I.'

Harker ignored Foster's gentle correction and said, 'What about here, in the hotel?'

72

'We saw them. At meals.'

'He was a very rude man,' said Foster.

'In what way?'

'He – er – he suggested that if the world goes mad – if there *is* a nuclear holocaust – I'd be responsible.'

'Raymond, darling, you didn't tell me that.' The shocked expression on her face wasn't make-believe.

Harker raised questioning eyebrows.

'I'm a physics master,' muttered Foster.

'That's pushing it a bit.'

'Darling, why didn't you *tell* me?'

'Let's get back to the time you were watching the gulls.'

'He'd no right to . . .'

'Please, Mrs Foster.'

'Raymond's been ill. Very ill. A remark like that . . .'

'It was a stupid remark, Mrs Foster. Not worth worrying about. Now, you recognised them as they walked along the path?'

'Yes.'

'*Recognised* them, Mrs Foster? It's no crime to be uncertain.'

'I thought I recognised them,' she said, then added, 'Then Raymond told me who they were.'

'And when she fell over the cliff?'

Foster walked to the window, stared out and said, 'She didn't *fall* over the cliff edge. She was *pushed*.'

'Darling, please don't . . .'

'Did you see it, Mrs Foster?' insisted Harker.

'No.' She was still watching her husband. 'Dear, you mustn't let it . . .'

'You *didn't* see it?'

'I saw he was alone.' She returned her attention to Harker. There was a quality of pleading in her eyes. 'I saw them walking along the path. Then I watched the gulls. Then . . .'

'Your husband had the binoculars?'

'Yes. But I'm not blind. I can still see . . .'

'First two? Then one?'

'Yes. He'd pushed her over the . . .'

'But *you* didn't see it?'

'Raymond saw it.'

73

'Then told you?'

'Yes.'

'But you didn't actually *see* it happen?'

'My husband doesn't tell lies, sergeant. Why should he?'

'No reason at all,' soothed Harker. 'I'm not calling him a liar. All I'm doing is digging for the truth. Making absolutely sure no mistakes have been made.'

'No mistakes!' Foster turned from the window. His face was pale, his eyes a little wild and he was trembling slightly. In a croaking voice he said, 'Why do you think it's taken me three days?'

'That's a question I'd like to . . .'

'Raymond dear, please don't. Don't get upset.'

'Making sure. Going over it, again and again. I don't enjoy accusing a man of murder. A man I don't even know.'

'But don't like,' murmured Harker.

'What has that to do with it? What has *that* to do with it? If you think I'm the sort of person who . . .'

'I think you're a very honest man,' said Harker calmly. 'Equally, I think your wife is a very honest woman. But even honest men make mistakes.'

'It's not a mistake!'

'Darling, please come and sit down. Please!'

They waited until Foster moved slowly across the carpet, then lowered himself onto the bed, alongside his wife. He gripped his knees, as if trying to tear the knee-caps loose. The slight trembling continued. Martha Foster placed a hand over one of his, as if to confirm the bond between them.

Harker gave them a few moments to settle then, in a calming tone, said, 'You did the right thing, Mr Foster. You thought things over, reached a decision, then reported what you'd seen. Fine. Let's assume you're right. That we're talking about murder. Saturday. It's now Tuesday. There's been an Inquest. The Coroner's recorded Death by Misadventure. Okay, a Coroner's verdict *can* be overturned, but it's not easy. Coroners are very important people. Most of them very self-important . . . which doesn't help.

'The forensic science people can't help. Where it happened. No footprints. Strictly speaking, too many footprints. The cliff-rescue crowd don't mess about. They've a job to do and they do it. They trample everywhere. The pathologist? He's performed a post mortem examination. Injuries consistent with falling down a cliff face and landing on rocks . . . which tells us nothing.

'Then, you trot along, and tell us what you have told us. Murder. That's what you tell us. That Duxbury pushed his wife over the edge. If you'd yelled, it might have helped. He might have panicked. It might have given us just that edge. But you didn't yell. You stayed behind the bushes. So, let's say you're right, Duxbury thinks he's got away with murder. It happens. Duxbury thinks it's happened this time. That's the only trump card we hold . . . that he thinks he's safe. You're it. The trump card. We have to make sure it *is* a trump card. Get as much weight behind it as we possibly can. It's not easy. It's not *going* to be easy.' He paused, then added, 'You see the problem?'

'He's got away with it,' muttered Foster.

'No. Not if we tread carefully.'

'I don't see how . . .'

'*My* job.' Harker pushed himself upright. 'You're here to recuperate. Relax. Long walks. Bags of sea air. Be guided by your wife. Right?'

Foster raised his head, and very solemnly said, 'Thank you.'

'For what?'

'For understanding. For believing me.'

The manager of the hotel was in his mid-fifties and grey haired. Being 'mine host' at a class hotel and restaurant – catering for people with money enough to complain if little things went wrong – made for ulcers, and the smile he wore when on duty was often very fixed. Part of the service, expected. Fun and games. Joviality. Eat, drink and be merry . . . and all that crap.

'Bad publicity,' he complained. 'Especially just before the Christmas rush. We could have done without it.'

'They forget,' soothed Harker.

'The hell they do! This is the hotel she was staying at when she fell over the cliff.'

'Not your fault.'

'*Everything's* my fault at this place. A thousand people *don't* fall over a cliff. That's not headline news. One does – just the one – and it's spread all over the front page of the local rag.' He sighed. 'You can't win, sergeant. There's no way out.'

They were in the manager's office. A large room. A roll-topped desk, a desk-chair, a slightly soiled armchair and two upright chairs. One wall was almost covered by a ruled rectangle of stiff paper; a detailed, see-at-a-glance run-down of dates, rooms, meals, functions, rotas . . . all the bits and pieces necessary for the behind-the-scenes running of a good hotel. A stringed batch of new brochures was on the carpet in one corner. A four-foot-high Chubb safe in another.

'Nice people?' asked Harker, off-handedly.

'Who?'

'The Duxburys?'

'Oh, sure. Very nice. Good class.'

'Friendly?'

'You should have seen them Friday night.' The manager permitted himself a quick, crooked smile. 'Laughing and joking with the other customers. I'm glad, in a way.'

'Glad?'

'Y'know . . . she had *one* good night, before the end.'

'One way of looking at it,' agreed Harker. He tasted the pink gin provided by the manager, then observed, 'Not a nice thing. Two happily married people, then one goes like that.'

'Fast, though.' The manager sipped at his own pink gin. 'I doubt if she suffered.'

'Who knows?' Harker frowned make-believe concern. 'It might not have been instantaneous.'

'True.' The manager nodded, sadly. 'I only hope so, for her sake.'

'Must have knocked him for six,' mused Harker.

'Duxbury?'

'He must have been in a hell of a state when he got back here.'

'Very upset. But bearing up. I rang for the rescue people. Then for his son.'

'I wonder . . .' Harker tapped the rubber furrel of the walking-stick on the carpet thoughtfully.

76

'What?'

'Why didn't he climb down to her? Check whether she was still alive?'

'It's the devil of a climb. And dangerous.'

'But his wife.'

'I know. But . . .'

'And happily married.'

'I don't think *I* would have done.'

'No?' Harker looked mildly surprised.

'I'd have done what he did. Hare for the nearest telephone.'

'Quite a way to run.'

'He was breathless. On the point of collapse. Flopped into a chair and gasped what had happened. *He* couldn't have telephoned. He could hardly speak.'

'I can believe you,' said Harker. 'What about the other residents? How did they take it?'

'The Fosters?'

'Whoever was there.'

'Only the Fosters and the Duxburys. It's a quiet period.'

'How did the Fosters take it?'

'As I recall . . .' The manager's expression gave the impression that he was screwing memory loose. 'They were out at the time. Came back about an hour later. Went straight to their room.'

'There'd be some excitement?'

'Of course.'

'But the – what's their name? – the Fosters weren't interested?'

'Young people.' The manager seemed to think the two words explained everything. He added, 'An odd couple.'

'Odd?'

'Fads. Fancies. Vegetarians. That sort of thing. A bit of a nuisance.'

'Y'mean rowdy?'

'Good Lord, no. No trouble that way. But ramming their silly notions down everybody's throat. I think they even tried Duxbury.'

'Oh, my word.'

'One of the porters heard them. Don't think they saw him. But, from what I'm told, Duxbury sent him away with a flea in his ear.'

'Not much love lost.'

'Shouldn't think so. Foster strikes me as a very broody type. Takes offence very easily.'

'Maybe that's why they weren't interested.'

'What?'

'When they got back. All the excitement, but they went up to their room.'

'I shouldn't wonder. Very self-centred. You know the type. Young. Know everything. Couldn't care less about common courtesies.'

Harker knew the trick. How to ask questions without *seeming* to ask questions. A chat – a passing of the time of day – but, within the sipping space of one pink gin, he learned a lot. A picture was being built up. Hazy. Not too much finer detail as yet. But it was coming. The Fosters. John Duxbury. Even Maude Duxbury. An empty space was gradually being filled.

As he rose to leave, he said, 'I'll have a word with the council. See about having that stretch of the cliff-edge railed off.'

'You'd be doing everybody a favour,' sighed the manager.

They walked along the cliff-edge slowly. This time they were not bird-watching. This time they were without binoculars or reference books. Just the two of them, with the man bent shouldered and with his head lowered until his chin was on his chest. With the woman gripping the loose ends of the nylon tie-string at the waist of his anorak, as if it was a life-line, without which and without her he might drift away from reality.

He stopped at the V in the edge, and she tightened her grip on the nylon cord. He stared at the bite in the cliff – at the thick sludge covering the path – oblivious to the plucking wind and the clouds of drizzling rain swept in from the sea.

'He *did* push her,' he muttered.

'Yes, Raymond dear.'

'Martha, he *did*.' He was pleading to be believed.

'Yes, dear. They're only . . .' She sought for the right words. 'They have to be sure. That's all.'

'I *am* sure.' Then in what amounted to a groan. 'It's going to be the same again.'

78

'No, dear.' Panic touched the quick denial.

'It is,' he insisted. 'Like at the school. The same again. I'll be called a liar. They'll humiliate me. They'll . . .'

'*They won't!*' She tugged at the cords, trying to pull him away from the edge. 'It's different this time. Murder. It's not like the other thing. Please, Raymond darling. *Please!*'

He resisted the tug and stood there motionless. His mind was filled and soured with a time not too long ago; with a court-room wherein simple truths were twisted and turned into petty vindictiveness; with a solicitor, and a cross-examination which, in effect, turned *him* into a wrong-doer.

'I won't go into a witness-box again,' he whispered. 'Not again.'

'Let's get back to the hotel Raymond, dear.'

'They can't *make* me.'

'Raymond, dear, let's go back to the hotel.'

The tug on the cords became more urgent. He turned, and together they walked slowly back along the path.

If the Sub-Divisional Headquarters building was ridiculous, the Divisional Headquarters building was sublime. You couldn't miss the place. Short of hiding behind corners, you couldn't help but *see* the place. Great controversy had raged when the site had been chosen. The controversy had heated up when the plans had become known, and when, in face of all public opposition, the damn place had been built the controversy had reached a fever pitch. And why not? A quiet little seaside town – a town which, over the years, had prided itself on retaining a relaxed, Olde Worlde image – and plumb in the centre a concrete filing-cabinet, three floors high, complete with flat roof and wireless mast. A very functional building; all right-angles and straight lines.

But who the hell cared about public opinion? The chief superintendent's office had its own private bathroom . . . and *that* was something few of the flash forces could boast!

The burghers of the town had come to accept the eyesore. They scowled as they passed. They knew they'd never pay for the infernal place in *their* lifetime, and that the cost of heating and lighting it would go on forever and ever, amen. But complaints can go on for only so long, and the local rag had long since stopped printing outraged prose in its Letters Column. So, like tower blocks in bigger towns and cities, the police D.H.Q. was viewed as a huge, irremovable wart, and the legacy from a not-so-long-ago age when size meant status.

Detective Sergeant Harry Harker rather liked the place. Plenty of room to spread out. No problem in keeping joint suspects well apart while you played he-says-this-so-why-don't-you-say-that games with them. And if, by chance, they made a run for it . . . so what? Without a street map they'd never find the front door!

He sprawled in a comfortable wing-chair, in the detective chief inspector's office, and fed facts and opinions to his immediate chief.

Detective Chief Inspector Briggs looked worried; as if he carried the cares of the world on his narrow shoulders. A man, thin to the point of gauntness, he'd learned the hard way. His exalted position was in no way due to this ability as a thief-taker, nor even his ability as a common-or-garden bobby. Some years back he'd married the assistant chief constable's daughter and, had he positioned himself on the launch pad at Cape Kennedy, his rise could not have been more certain or more spectacular. Which is okay, and one way of reaching dizzy heights, just as long as you don't retain the mental outlook of a door-knob-trier. That was Brigg's burden. He was secretly (and sometimes not so secretly) terrified of the rank. He loathed taking responsibility, but at the same time had to tread carefully and not pass too many cans. The A.C.C. wasn't a popular man, and a whole army of flatfeet were gunning for him, if necessary via his son-in-law.

Added to which Briggs had sense enough to realise that any one of the three detective sergeants under his immediate command could police him off the face of the earth . . . and, of the three, Harker was the daddy.

'You've got to have *some* idea,' he pleaded.

Harker held out a hand and rocked it from side to side.

'Do *you* think it's murder?' insisted Briggs.

'Foster says so.'

'And?'

H E 'Him and his wife were bird watching at the time.'

'What does the wife say?'

80

'She claims her husband always tells the truth.'

'So, that means . . .'

'That's what *she* says.'

'Oh, my Christ!'

The truth was, Harker rather enjoyed getting Briggs hot and bothered. He didn't dislike the chief inspector; he was harmless enough; given time, he could be jollied into agreeing that up was down. But (hell's teeth!) the salary he was drawing for doing damn-all. That rankled a little.

'Harry,' said Briggs patiently, 'come on. Don't fool around. I need to know. Do I squash it or do I get the big wheel turning?'

'Well, now.' Harker settled himself more comfortably in the wing-chair. 'Let's take it for granted that Duxbury insists she fell. That leaves Foster as sole witness. He was watching gulls at the time. Had binoculars to his eyes and was following the flight of one of the gulls. Suddenly, Duxbury comes into focus pushing – or having just pushed – his missus over the edge. Duxbury didn't know he was being watched.'

'So, it's murder?'

'On the other hand,' continued Harker calmly, 'Foster and his missus didn't act as if they'd just witnessed a murder. No yelling. No shouting. Just lying doggo, pending the murderer making himself scarce. *And* – when they did move – it wasn't to the nearest nick, or to a telephone. Back to the hotel. A smart nip up to their room. Then *three days* before Foster decides wife-killing isn't the done thing.'

'Ah, so it's *not* murder?'

'Isn't it?' asked Harker innocently.

'You've as good as said . . .'

'Facts. That's what I'm reporting. And another fact worth considering. *If* she fell, Duxbury wasn't in any blind hurry to get help. Ten minutes – maybe a quarter of an hour – he just stood there, looking down at her. Could be a reason. Could be a very nasty reason.'

'Anything else?' sighed Briggs.

'Likes and dislikes. The hotel manager liked the Duxburys, but doesn't like the Fosters. There wasn't much love lost between the Fosters and the Duxburys. That's what it boils down to. That's what we have to go on.' Harker slipped the half-hunter from his waistcoat pocket and, very pointedly, checked the time. 'Generally speaking, a chuffed-up day. We haven't really moved from square one.'

'A murder enquiry?' Then in near desperation, 'Harry – for Christ's sake! – is it or isn't it?'

Harker returned the watch to its pocket, then said, 'Some nut case waltzes into a local nick and says murder's been committed. We can't call him a liar. On the other hand – especially when the Coroner's had his say – we can't fire off distress rockets, just on his say-so. Somebody's lying. Somebody's mistaken. Somebody's having us on. Maybe a mix of all three. You have problems, chief inspector. Pull the plug, and the Coroner will start asking awkward questions. It'll make *him* look a bit of a Charlie. Sling the complaint into the nearest waste-paper basket and, if Foster repeats his complaint somewhere else, you could have a real rocket tied to your tail. *And* some smart boyo just might have committed murder on this patch, and walked away from it . . . and *he* might get a skinful in the not too distant future and start telling his pals how dumb we all are.'

'What would *you* do?' whispered Briggs.

'I take orders.' Harker grinned mischievously. 'You're the lad drawing the pay.'

'Please, Harry.'

'Okay.' Harker nodded slowly. 'Use all the weight you have. Sit on it for a few days, and hope to God it doesn't hatch. Meanwhile, I'll nose around . . . all expenses paid, of course. I'll try to find the liar. When I'm sure – moderately sure – I'll report back. Meanwhile, just us two.'

'Thanks. Thanks a lot.'

'You've damn-all to thank me for yet.'

Harker hoisted himself from the chair and gripped his walking-stick.

As he reached the door, Briggs said, 'I'll not forget this, Harry. You have my word. I'll not forget.'

'Don't worry . . . I'll keep reminding you.'

* * *

82

She held him like a mother holding a frightened child. Periodically he trembled and when he did her arms tightened a little in assurance. It was cool between the sheets, but she could feel the heat from his body, and that was all she asked for. To know he was there. To know that, for the moment at least, *he* needed *her*.

He wasn't a liar. He hadn't lied the last time. Never mind the verdict of the court, this man of hers *couldn't* lie. He was too wise, but at the same time too innocent. Stupid policemen! They hadn't the vision to recognise a truly *good* man when they met one. Theirs was a crazy world, a wicked world filled with suspicion and doubt. How could they understand? How could they know the meaning of honour and absolute honesty?

PART THREE

The Diary of John Duxbury

This diary is my life-line. It stretches from the past to the present and, hopefully, into the future. But what sort of future? A future without Maude. But what sort of a future is that? Empty? I don't yet know. Certainly a future with something missing. A future with a space which can never be re-filled.

No more wives! Nobody else to be granted the right to humiliate me, as the whim takes her.

I wish I hadn't penned those words, Harry. She was your mother. She loved you and (rightly) you returned that love. Perhaps I was jealous. Jealous of the affection she had for you. Certain it is that your birth changed things. You never knew that, did you? But I think you should know. I was 'driven out', if that is not too dramatic a way of putting it. She seemed to resent *my* love for you. As if the conception had been hers, and hers alone. As if I had no *right* to love you. As if I was a stranger, making a nuisance of myself in showing love for a child not his.

Had it been any other woman . . .

Have no doubts about it, Harry. I'm your father. No other man. Maude had faults, but infidelity was certainly not one of them.

This afternoon I tried to read. *The Mask of Dimitrios.* Even Eric Ambler couldn't hold me. Couldn't push the memories aside long enough to ease the hurt a little. Perhaps because we saw the film together in happier times. Sidney Greenstreet and Peter Lorre . . . but I can't remember the name of the actor who portrayed Dimitrios. We saw the film and enjoyed it and, in those days, shared enjoyment.

I couldn't read. I tried the hi-fi, thinking that music might do what words couldn't do, but it was no good. Eventually, I went for a walk along the surrounding lanes. It merely increased the isolation. Proved how lonely I was. I found myself talking. Talking quietly to myself, but (God help me!) pretending that Maude was with me, and that she was listening.

I miss her. Had you asked me once upon a time – even weeks ago – I would have denied it. I might have said we all have to die at some time. I might even have laughed and claimed, with as near certainty as possible, that *I* would die first. I would have brushed this possibility aside, but secretly I might also have toyed with the idea of what I would then have called 'freedom'.

Freedom!

I think what freedom I have is rather like that of an escaped animal born and brought up in captivity. The freedom of not knowing which way to turn. The freedom of being lost and not a little afraid.

I wish . . .

The pantomime season is upon us and, if ever there was such a thing as a good fairy, I would not ask for three wishes. One would suffice. To reverse time a mere week, knowing what I now know. The walk along that cliff-edge would not take place. The fatal walk. When she went over, screaming. When I stood, looking down at her. God! Knowing what I now know. The loneliness. The helplessness. Those moments of sheer panic when full realisation takes over the whole mind, and blots out all other thoughts.

Maude! Maude! Why did you turn me against you so many times? Why did you sadden me so? Why did you change?

Don't let it happen, Harry. Not to you and Ben. Fight for happiness. Beg for it. Pay any price for it. Anything. The everlasting switchback of misery and mediocrity is no way to live. Not when you've touched the heights. Not when you *know* the other thing. Keep happiness, whatever the cost.

Above all, keep it together . . .

Last night, I dreamed. A fitful sleep, having recorded my thoughts and the happenings of the day. Nevertheless, I dreamed. A nightmare in which Maude returned, but not the same Maude. A Maude mad for vengeance. Her hair was straight and wet, with strands of seaweed clinging to her head and neck. Her mouth was wide, and the grey scum of washed-up foam dripped from her lips. She was dead . . . but *not* dead.

I think I awakened myself by screaming. Perhaps. I know I was terrified. I switched on every light in the bedroom, but still I trembled and still my mind would not rid itself of the horror. My pyjamas were soaked with sweat, and I went to the bathroom and showered. Then I dressed. Nothing would have induced me to try to sleep again after that dream.

It was four o'clock. Not yet light. The house was cold. The central heating system had not yet switched itself on. I brewed tea, smoked my pipe and re-lived the dream again and again . . . couldn't rid myself of it. It was a haunting. Nothing less. A haunting, and I am frightened to leave this diary and go to my bed, because the haunting may come again.

Ghosts? No, of course I don't believe in ghosts. Ghosts are figments of the imagination. That (or as Scrooge insisted) a piece of undigested cheese. But if they *are* a figment of the imagination they are real enough to haunt the brain and, if they haunt the brain, they exist. What are dreams, if they are not hauntings? What are the creatures of dreams, if not ghosts? They don't exist. Like ghosts, they don't exist . . . but when they come they're real enough!

Shortly after first light, I drove out to the Tops. High above the world, where the cold air and the bleak landscape can banish (albeit temporarily) every ghost that ever walked.

I left the car and walked. Walked until I was chilled to the bone. Then I returned to the car, and drove until I found an isolated inn where I enjoyed a bar snack. I found what I think I needed. Good people. Honest people. Down-to-earth Yorkshire folk, ready to laugh and yarn together. I kept apart, but listened. I even smiled at some of the gentle, meaningless insults bandied around.

Whole people. Complete people. Complete, as I think *I* never will be again.

And still I felt guilty because Maude might not have approved. Might still not approve. Might return tonight to scream her disapproval.

I wonder. Can anybody know how I felt while I drove back from the Tops? I, John Duxbury, the owner of a successful printing firm, who'd started with nothing, dragged himself up by the boot-straps, done nobody a deliberate injury . . . and now? Less than a man. A creature terrified of sleep. Somebody not too far from true madness.

Almost on an impulse I called at the locum's and wheedled myself an immediate appointment. I needed a doctor. I needed *somebody!* And yet, I couldn't tell him everything. Bits and pieces. A few disjointed, meaningless sentences which merely puzzled him. 'Was I sleeping badly?' That was one question he asked. His exact words. I could answer truthfully. I was sleeping *very* badly, but not the way *he* meant, and not for the reasons *he* thought. He gave me some Sodium Amytol capsules. Assured me that a couple, at bedtime, would make me sleep like a child. I hope so. I hope children don't have dreams or nightmares. I hope so many things.

SATURDAY, 11TH DECEMBER

A sleep-filled, dreamless night, but paid for by a throbbing head this morning. It eased by noon, and I felt refreshed by the sleep. I was able to sit down and, with comparative objectivity, think of what I had and what I no longer had.

Maude. I no longer have Maude. Understand me, Harry, she was a good mother. A fine mother. But as a wife (at least in the last few years) she left much to be desired. She wasn't a *friend*. That, I think, is important. Simple friendship, companionship if you like, is a vital part of a good marriage, and that she wouldn't give me. She was demanding. She was spoiled and, as she grew older, she grew more and more like a spoiled child. I was sometimes driven to the conclusion that she'd come to view marriage as an easy way to obtain the luxuries of life. She dominated me. I make no secret of that. Nor do I make excuses. She had the upper hand, because wherever we were, and whatever the circumstances, she 'spoke her mind'. Her own expression. Often, it was a handy excuse for down-right ill-temper and bad manners.

She was always 'right'. (I list her faults first, then I'll list her good points and, finally, I'll list my own faults . . . if, that is, a man can be objective enough to see *all* his faults.) But even when she was monumentally wrong, even when everybody else pointed out how wrong she was, she doggedly remained 'right'. Nor was it just an expressed opinion. She often stated the most silly conclusions as proven facts, merely because *she* had voiced them. Eventually, of course, people dismissed what she said as the ramblings of a biased person. But I had to live with it, and it wasn't easy. I never argued. I'd learned that argument and logic were wasted. You agreed with her, or you were a fool. Therefore . . . silence. No argument. It went in at one ear and came out at the other.

It cost us friends. Good friends. Even the best of friends can only stand so much irritable nonsense. Serious conversation became impossible, and people grew tired of making excuses.

Gradually, then, a joyless, rootless marriage. And, to be honest, I think Maude was as unhappy as I was. I'm sure she was, but didn't know why. A stronger man might have salvaged something. Held out against her. Forced her to alter her ways. but as far as Maude was concerned I'd been too weak too long. I couldn't change my ways without . . .

I started this entry at late evening, and I was interrupted by the telephone bell. Harry, telling me that some policeman (a detective sergeant) from the district where Maude died has visited the firm. Asking questions. Hints that the Coroner isn't quite satisfied. Small points which need clearing up. What small points? What sort of questions, and to whom asked? God, will this thing never end?

PART FOUR

The Enquiries of Harry Harker

David Shaw, B.A. (Oxon) hated Wednesdays. The fourth day of the week and Woden's day; a Germanic day if ever there was one and, as a rule, Wagnerian in its general melodramatic shambles. That clown of a Youth Employment Officer usually 'popped in' on a Wednesday. God only knew why. He merely spread gloom and despondency. The sixteen- and seventeen-year-olds – the yobs who thought they were already men and women – hadn't a cat in hell's chance of a decent job once they were hurled from the cosy womb of the school. Check-out-point fodder at some supermarket most of them. *And* all they were good for. The bright sparks were already earmarked for further education. But this over-optimistic idiot seemed to hold a secret belief that a comprehensive school of almost 2000 pupils was a forcing shed for future brain surgeons and the like. 'Tell me, headmaster. That youth I passed who'd just come from your study. He has the air of an individualist. Would he be interested in the post of assistant stage manager at the local theatre?' That had been last week. And – presumably as the Youth Employment Officer knew – an A.S.M. was a person with Thespian ambitions . . . and 'that youth' was hardly able to mumble his own name! And on Wednesdays the catering manageress presented the proposed menu for the coming week's meals, complete with complaints and suggestions. 'Couldn't we call it something other than Spotted Dick, Mr Shaw? It sounds so unappetising.' '*They'll* still call it Spotted Dick.' 'Worse . . . *they* call it "Dead Baby".' 'Do they eat it?' 'Most of them do.' 'As I suspected. They're all cannibals at heart.'

And to think that he'd once enjoyed being a schoolmaster. More than enjoyed it. He'd viewed every pupil as a budding genius;

worked himself to the point of exhaustion hammering home facts and figures, the subtle differences between good and mediocre literature, the beauty of fine poetry, the sweep of history, the magnificence of great art.

In those days . . .

Or had kids *always* been miniature ogres? Had they *always* had strip-cartoon pop-music mentalities? He thought not. In those days you taught them. These days you *trained* them, like so many half-wild animals. Two thousand of the little horrors and, every day, a handful of them would be marched to his desk for what passed as 'punishment'. A talking to. A letter to their parents. An appeal to a better nature they didn't possess. Whereas in the old days six of the best across the tightened britches of a bent backside ensured that the recipient got the message loud and clear: that he was at school to learn.

Shaw was a soured, disillusioned man and, as he entered the outer office he grunted a morning greeting to his over-worked secretary.

She stopped typing, looked up and said, 'There's a Detective Sergeant Harker waiting in your office, headmaster.'

'Who?'

'A Detective Sergeant Harker. I asked him to wait in your office.'

'What the devil have they been up to this time?'

'I really don't . . .'

'Rustle up some coffee, please. And see we're not disturbed.'

Shaw strode across the room, entered his office and closed the door. Harker rose from the chair he'd been sitting in, and they shook hands.

As he lowered himself into the desk chair, Shaw waved Harker to sit down again, and said, 'Detective Sergeant Harker?'

Harker nodded and settled his walking stick more comfortably alongside his leg.

'Who?' asked Shaw bluntly. 'And what has he, she – or they – been up to?'

'Not the pupils.' Harker smiled.

'That makes a pleasant change.'

'One of your masters. A Mr Foster. Raymond Foster.'

'He's not here.' The hint of a frown touched Shaw's brow.

'I know. I spoke to him yesterday.'

'In that case . . .'

'I want to know *about* him,' said Harker calmly.

'About him?'

'As much as possible. As much as you're prepared to tell me.'

Shaw picked a pencil from the desk top, sucked the end meditatively for a moment, then murmured, 'You have proof of identity, of course?'

Harker took his wallet from an inside pocket of his jacket, slipped out his warrant card and slid it across the desk.

Shaw glanced at it and said, 'Not from the local force.'

'From where Foster's holidaying.'

'Ah!' Shaw returned the warrant card.

'He's not in trouble.' Harker progressed slowly – carefully – as he returned the warrant card and wallet to its pocket. 'He's made a complaint. A serious complaint. We're checking it out.'

'A complaint about here? About this school?'

'No. About something he claims he saw.'

'Flying saucers?' There was sardonic impatience in the question.

'Would he?' asked Harker solemnly.

'What?'

'Claim to have seen flying saucers?'

'You've been to the local police, of course?'

'Of course,' lied Harker.

'In that case, you'll know about him and Flemming.'

'Of course.' Harker repeated the lie.

'It should never have happened.'

'Didn't it happen?' fished Harker.

'I've no doubt it did . . . knowing Flemming. Despite the verdict. But we could have kept it within the limits of the school. Instead . . . a lot of bad publicity, and Flemming got away with it.'

'Foster's fault, of course?'

'He shouldn't have gone to the police. Not without consulting me first.'

'From your angle.' Harker moved a hand, as if to suggest that it wasn't *too* important. 'The official angle. I know that, of course.

97

But what *you* thought. What *you* think happened?'

'Oh, Flemming was messing about with this senior girl in the science lab. I don't doubt that for a moment. And when Foster walked in and saw them . . .' Shaw blew out his cheeks. 'It happens. Young masters. Some of the girls egg them on. But he shouldn't have sent for the police. "Citizen's Arrest"! Good God . . . what next? The first I knew about it was when the police car arrived. It made me look a bit of a fool.'

'The sort of thing he'd do?' asked Harker innocently. 'Foster, I mean.'

'The most unpredictable man I've ever met.' Then hurriedly, 'Knows his subject, I'll say that for him. Physics. He stands in for maths or science sometimes. Even biology, at a pinch. But he should never have been a schoolmaster.'

'Between these walls,' murmured Harker. 'Nothing "official".'

'Mmm.' Shaw hesitated.

'Nothing on paper,' urged Harker. 'Nothing repeated.'

Shaw said, 'He has the wrong personality.'

'To be a schoolmaster?'

'To have even considered the teaching profession.' Shaw seemed to reach a decision, he leaned forward fractionally, then continued, 'Sergeant, this job of encouraging the youth of today to learn. It would make old-time company sergeant majors weep tears of frustration. This is a good school. *I* see to that. But ask the average pupil to name the author of *Alice in Wonderland*. Ask him, or her, to say how many symphonies Beethoven composed. Ask which Emperor of Rome Augustus was. The motto of the Order of the Garter. Ask a hundred similar, simple questions, and you'll get a blank stare. They don't know. They don't *want* to know. As far as they're concerned that's all useless knowledge. But ask which lunatic group topped the pop charts this week, last week, last month. Ask which idiot produced or directed the latest science fiction movie. Ask which is the bluest comedian to be let loose on a television screen. Who's the most ill-tempered tennis player in the world. Which footballer plays the dirtiest game. *Those* things they know. Those priceless gems of knowledge they carefully store in their brain. And *that*, sergeant, is the wall of moronic stupidity every schoolmaster – every schoolmistress – must either climb or

98

demolish before he, or she, can even start to enthuse about the subject to be taught. In short, it is a fight – almost open warfare – between the class and the teacher most of the time. And the teacher must win. He must impose his will upon the class, otherwise he's wasting his time. Determination and discipline. Together in the right quantities they command respect. Given respect, something approximating knowledge can be imparted.'

'Not Foster?' Harker half-smiled as he spoke.

'They are horrors.' It was Wednesday, therefore Shaw warmed to his subject. 'I speak generally, of course, but of the majority. God, in His infinite wisdom, knows what sort of citizens they'll become. This school – a good school – is nevertheless like all other present day schools, a jungle. And there is no place in a jungle for men like Foster. Given half a chance he could teach these louts mysteries which, unfortunately, will remain well beyond their limited comprehension for the rest of their miserable lives. But they haven't the sense to let him. They rag him. They mock him. They make him miserable . . . and take perverted pleasure in so doing. I have watched him at the end of a day's work. Often. A beaten man. A man almost reduced to tears, because he refuses to *demand* that they learn.' He paused, looked saddened, then went on, 'It was coming. The incident with Flemming – the court case – merely hastened it. A nervous breakdown. Utter mental exhaustion.' Another pause, then, 'Sergeant, you think *you* deal with the villains of this world. Believe me, nobody – nobody! – can be more cruel than children en masse when they have an adult at their mercy.'

The coffee came and, as they sipped it, Shaw smoked a battered pipe and (probably because it was Wednesday) expanded upon the same theme. A possible exaggeration here and there. A determination to convince Harker that teaching was the most soul-destroying job on God's earth. He moved from the specifics of Foster to generalities and Harker interrupted but rarely. The object was to get an assessment of Foster and, at the same time, get an assessment of the assessor. The tactics of a cunning and very experienced copper.

'Flemming?' murmured Harker, as Shaw paused to re-light his pipe.

99

'Out of it. Round Bristol way somewhere. Let somebody else worry about *him*.'

'He was aquitted.'

'By the court. Not by me. One of these modern, first-name-all-pals-together masters. A "toucher" – you know the kind, can't keep their hands to themselves. I had a quiet word with the Education Committee.'

'As easy as that?' Harker looked mildly surprised.

'I, too, convinced him that in his own interests he should apply for the other job.'

'Very persuasive,' observed Harker.

'Who?'

'You. My immediate impression.'

'Nor are *you* a fool,' countered Shaw. '*My* immediate impression.'

'Oh, I'm just a run-of-the-mill detective sergeant,' protested Harker. 'I do my job, draw my cheque . . . not much else.'

Shaw chuckled quietly – knowingly – and held a newly lighted match to the surface of the tobacco in the bowl of his pipe.

They sat in silence for a few moments, each sipping coffee and each waiting for the next move. Both were wise enough to know the meeting was not yet over; over that other questions had to be asked and answered. Beyond the window it had started to rain and puddles were forming on the uneven patches of the tarmac stretch which surrounded the school. From inside the school – from beyond the secretary's office – a bell sounded, followed by the distant clatter of running feet.

'Foster is no disciplinarian,' said Harker at last.

'To put it mildly.'

'Unpopular?'

'Oddly enough, no.' Shaw puffed at this pipe then continued, 'The mind of a teenager. Give it a stupidity, and it will latch onto it and make it a cult. And Foster is a mass of stupidities.'

Harker raised a questioning eyebrow.

'Vegetarianism,' explained Shaw. 'Agnosticism. Anti-pollution. The brotherhood of man. Sex equality. You name it. If it's hairbrained enough Foster's an advocate. The kids know this. It's a novelty. They'll listen to his every word. What they *won't* listen to is the subject he's here to teach.'

100

'Surely, if he can get them interested in one thing . . .' Harker left the remark open-ended.

'He hasn't the knack.' Shaw sighed. 'He won't slap any of them down. Physically or verbally. They take advantage . . . and he's hurt. Damnation, he's popular. Correction, he *could* be popular.'

'And yet you say you've seen him almost weeping.'

'The various "isms",' grunted Shaw, still with the stem of his pipe clenched between his teeth. 'That, plus other things. He hurts too readily. His skin's no thicker than rice paper and in this job you need elephant hide. The kids. This nuclear-age generation. They vandalise for the sake of vandalism . . . and that includes the feelings of people. Even people they like. Sergeant Harker.' The tone became less brusque. The eyes took on a slight faraway look. 'Our generation. A personal opinion. We're the last of the romantics. I see them. I live with them. The so-called "future". Most of them don't go out of their way to be even decent . . . much less polite. Give them somebody like Foster, and they have a ball. Not because they dislike him. Because he's there, and because he's vulnerable. For some crazy reason they don't seem to be able to stop themselves . . . and men like Foster leave themselves wide open and won't fight back.'

'The last of the romantics,' murmured Harker.

'That word "love",' mused Shaw sadly. 'They reserve it for pop stars. Movie idols. Occasionally an animal . . . a dog, a cat, a horse. But hardly ever for other human beings with whom they come in contact. They're missing out on something very important. They're only half-alive, but don't know it.'

Shaw fished a knife from his pocket, opened a thin blade and began to tease the damp dottle from the bowl of the pipe into a large glass ash-tray on his desk top.

As he fiddled the last few strands clear of the bowl he said, 'Am I allowed to ask a question?'

'Why not?'

'Your reason for being here. Your *real* reason.'

'A woman died.' Harker spoke a little slower than usual. Slowly and carefully. 'She went over a cliff edge. The inquest brought in a verdict of Accidental Death. Foster says she was pushed.'

'Oh, my God!'

'He kept quiet until after the inquest.'

101

'Foster all over.' Shaw frowned his impatience. He pushed himself from the chair, walked to the window and watched the worsening weather for a moment. 'He either goes off at half-cock or dithers around until he ends up making a fool of himself.' He turned his head, looked at Harker, and said, 'He *has* made a fool of himself?'

'He should have told us sooner.' There was only mild censure in the words.

'And now it's too late.' Shaw returned his attention to the weather. 'One more scoundrel gets away with murder. Or was there more than one?'

'Just the one . . . if there *was* one.'

'If?' Shaw turned from the window. 'You said . . .'

'The Coroner's verdict was Accidental Death.'

'Nevertheless, if murder's been committed . . .'

'It might have been,' said Harker flatly.

'Only "might" now?'

'We only have Foster's word. His version. And he was bird watching at the time.'

'He doesn't lie,' said Shaw bluntly.

'We all make mistakes.' Harker smiled. 'It's a one-and-one situation. His word against another man's.'

'No other witnesses?'

'No. Mrs Foster was there, but she didn't see it.'

'No evidence?'

'Only what Foster says.'

'He'll tell the truth.' Shaw compressed his lips. 'I'll stake my life on that, sergeant. He'll tell the truth, but it won't *sound* like the truth.'

Harker saw no reason at all to live rough or skimp things. This trip outside his own force area was being made at the personal request of the son-in-law of the A.C.C. no less. A large and juicy chestnut was teetering on the hob, ready to topple into white-hot embers and, if it fell, a certain Detective Chief Inspector Briggs was likely to have burned fingers for the rest of his life.

Well, if so, hard cheese. Harry Harker, Esq. wouldn't lose much sleep. Briggs was a prize nerk, and prize nerks were there to get their fingers scorched.

Meanwhile . . .

'I'll start with a prawn cocktail.' Harker glanced up from the menu and at the solemn-faced waiter. 'Then for main course, pheasant in Bordeaux, with all the trimmings.'

'Yes, sir.' The waiter noted the order on his pad.

'Half a bottle of decent wine.'

'I'll send the wine waiter over, sir.'

'Fair enough. Then for dessert, *apfelstrudel*. Coffee, cheese and biscuits.'

'Thank you sir.'

The waiter glided across the thick-piled carpet, and Harker viewed his fellow-lunchers. A very Ritzy joint. Very well patronised. Mostly well-dressed men. Middle-management types enjoying business lunches paid for by the firm. A smooth-talking con merchant, perhaps? Somebody with his hand well and truly in the till? Even a murderer?

It was a game Harker played. In modern parlance it was called 'body language', but working policemen had known it and used it for years. The tiny signs. The cigarette being smoked a little too jerkily and without real enjoyment. The continual dabbing of the mouth with a napkin; the mouth and the upper lip to remove the hint of saliva and the sheen of sweat. The barrier of the arm across the edge of the table; the token 'wall' beyond which nobody must trespass. The smile which didn't reach as far as the eyes. The knife and fork held just a mite awkwardly; as if they were weapons of defence.

The wine waiter came and went. The prawn cocktail arrived.

Harker continued his cogitations as he ate.

Murder. Murderers.

A man – a woman – capable of murder has nerve. The act itself, especially when committed in cold blood, calls for a certain twisted courage. The so-called 'perfect' murder – never detected, never even detected as *murder*. That, perhaps, was its fascination. The reason why – fact or fiction – it was the most written about crime of them all. A two-layer detection. Every living thing dies. Every man. Every woman. The vast majority die because their life has come to a natural end. Others die because of accidents. But the rest? Suicide accounts for some. But even so the tally is incomplete. How many Death Certificates? How many inquests? How many sighs of relief?

How many murders not *recognised* as murders? How many murders, recognised as murders, but with no hope of proof? The permutations are endless. Murderers – murderers *known* to be murderers – walk the streets and nod polite greeting to passing coppers . . . and damn-all can be done about it.

Harker chewed his way slowly through an excellent meal and allowed his thoughts to touch upon these questions, knowing there were no real answers.

Slowly, an anger grew inside him. Shaw had been so sure, and Shaw was no fool. With all his faults, Foster wasn't a liar. And if Foster wasn't a liar, that meant that Duxbury *was* a murderer. Discounting mistakes – and, for the moment Harker discounted the possibility that Foster had made a mistake – Duxbury had killed his wife and got away with it. Briggs wasn't important any more. Briggs was a clown dog who held rank he wasn't entitled to. What mattered – what *really* mattered – was the fact that Duxbury had committed murder on his (Harker's) patch. Had committed murder and was, no doubt, congratulating himself. He'd pulled it off. 'The Big One' . . . and he'd pulled it off.

The hell he had!

Harker paid his bill, asked for and received a receipt, hobbled to the hat-stand to collect his walking stick, his mac and his hat, then made his way to the parked Fiesta.

Many organisations claim to be 'The Most Select Club in the World'. Parliament, the Lords Taverners, the Bench, the Bar, top class public schools . . . and that not counting a handful of oak-panelled, male-orientated mausoleums within the boundaries of the City of London. But ask a copper with a modicum of service beneath the soles of his shoes and he (or even she) won't hesitate. The British Police Service. They need no ties, no passwords, no fancy handshakes. A good copper recognises a fellow-copper of similar stature within minutes. The speech, the manner, the hint of cynicism, the natural phraseology used throughout the service to describe certain circumstances and certain types.

Harker recognised Beechwood and was satisfied. They were of a rank – each a detective sergeant – although not of an age. Harker was at least ten years older than Beechwood and, whereas

Beechwood was slim and obviously very fit, Harker was thickset, limped a little and tended to become breathless very easily. Nevertheless, they were both working jacks and could count beans up to and including five.

'My case,' said Beechwood. 'Flemming should have gone down.'

They were in a C.I.D. Office and, like most C.I.D. Offices, it was a large room, over-filled with desks, filing cabinets, typewriters and (of course!) paper. Because he was a sergeant, Beechwood was allowed one corner of the office; a space no larger than the average boxroom in which he was expected to perform minor miracles of lesser administration, plus the general run of crime detection. Beechwood had a buttock on a corner of his desk, while Harker sat in the swivel chair and slowly turned his walking stick.

'Gone down?' Harker sounded genuinely surprised.

'Christ, yes. She was a little cow, game for the whole hog, and Flemming was *going* the whole hog until Foster opened the door.

'Rape?'

'A damn sight more than feelie-for-feelie.'

'So, why just Indecent Assault?'

'One of those things.' Beechwood moved a hand in disgust. 'The silly little bitch hummed and hawed in her statement. Maybe it wasn't *quite* rape, but it would have been if Foster had had difficulty opening the door. So, we played safe. Went for the cert, and he should have gone down.'

'What went wrong?' asked Harker.

'The girl was a lousy witness. Didn't want to give evidence. Then Foster blew it completely.'

'Foster?'

'Quince gave him hell under cross-examination. We'd warned him – Foster, I mean – just say "Yes" or "No" or "I don't know". Instead, he started to qualify his answers. "In my opinion this." "In my opinion that." Quince crucified him.'

'As bad as that?'

'Mate, a stranger coming into that courtroom would have thought *Foster* was on trial. He was damn near in tears when he left the box.'

The door of the C.I.D. Office opened and a detective constable ushered a man topping him by a good three inches into the room.

Beechwood called, 'Was he in the Wimpy Bar?'

'Where else?' The D.C. grinned his obvious delight and guided the large man to a chair at one of the desks.

Beechwood returned his attention to Harker, and growled, 'A clothes-line cowboy.'

'Women's frillies?'

'I've yet to know of 'em pinching a pair of long johns.'

'Quince?' Harker jerked the conversation back to its original subject.

'A solicitor. Damn good bloke. He can cross-examine better than most barristers.'

'That's not saying a hell of a lot.'

'As you remark.' Beechwood gave a quick, twisted smile.

They were two professionals, assessing the capabilities of their opponents. Each with experience of courtroom tactics; each aware that the Presumption of Innocence, while being a corner-stone of the British Legal System could, in the hands of a skilled advocate, screw up the best case in the world if prosecution witnesses waffled.

Harker twiddled the walking stick and murmured, 'He says he witnessed a murder.'

'Who? Foster?'

'A man pushing his wife over a cliff edge. No other witnesses. No forensic back-up.'

Beechwood blew out his cheeks.

'He kept his mouth shut for three days . . . until after the inquest. The Coroner's verdict was Accidental Death.'

'Jesus wept!'

'I think he's telling the truth,' said Harker flatly.

'Could be, but I wouldn't like to be in your shoes.'

'I've seen his boss,' said Harker heavily. 'The headmaster at the school where he works. I'm told he's *not* a liar.'

'True enough.' Beechwood rubbed the nape of his neck. 'He told the truth in the Flemming case.'

'But a bad witness?'

'I've never known a worse.'

'Something about a nervous breakdown.'

'Uhu.' Beechwood nodded and continued to rub the back of his neck. 'Highly strung. That sort. I think the beating he took from

106

Quince pushed him over the edge.'

'Y'know,' rumbled Harker, 'I'm beginning to dislike this Quince character.'

'He did what he was paid to do,' said Beechwood.

'He wasn't paid to let a murderer walk away scot-free.'

'He wouldn't know that, of course.'

Harker snorted.

'Dammit, mate,' protested Beechwood, 'you can't . . .'

'I can! I *do*.' Harker's anger rose. 'Smart-arse lawyers. They know their client's as guilty as hell. They know nine witnesses out of ten haven't even seen the inside of a courtroom. It's a game, played on *their* midden. Hell's teeth, isn't that enough? Do they have to smash an honest man until he's no good to the police any more? That's not "presenting a case". That's screwing up the law. Screwing up justice. We come up against too many "Quinces" in this job.'

'I'm sorry,' muttered Beechwood. 'I wish I could help.'

'Who's Foster's medic?' Harker quietened his temper.

'Er . . .' Beechwood hesitated as he rummaged through his memory, then said, 'Dr Nape-Smith.'

'Know him?'

'Fairly well.'

'Can you fix me an off-the-record appointment with him, for this evening?'

'I think so. I can try.' Beechwood reached for the telephone.

Harker walked the pavements, slowly and with simmering disgust. The rain had eased, but the damp atmosphere made his smashed foot ache like the very devil and this, too, added to his angry impatience.

Murder. For Christ's sake *murder*. Simple, uncomplicated, premeditated murder, committed on *his* stamping ground and in front of a witness . . . and the bastard was going to get away with it! This Duxbury – this John Duxbury – was having luck. Luck by the ton. A three-day start. A Coroner who'd already made up his mind. At a pinch the corpse already disposed of. And the one witness – the only witness – some clown who crumpled under cross-examination. Foster. As weak as water. As reliable as a plastic lemon. It had to be *him*. Not even him and his wife. Just Foster and a passing glance through a pair of binoculars while he was watching a bloody bird he couldn't even recognise.

Nobody should have such luck. Nobody should be *allowed* such luck.

And Duxbury?

Who the hell *was* Duxbury? What sort of a man? What sort of an animal who could push a woman – push his wife – to her death from a cliff top?

Odd, he didn't have any doubts left. Having talked to the hotel manager, before he'd set out on this crazy trip at Briggs's suggestion, he hadn't had much doubt. Foster had been talking out of the back of his neck. But Shaw and Beechwood had changed all that. They *knew* Foster; knew him a sight better than the hotel manager knew him. And they were sure. Foster didn't tell lies. Ever! He was every sort of an idiot, but not a lying idiot. Therefore . . .

The swing of the pendulum. A swing the wrong way and a very firm swing. A state of not having *much* doubt to a state of having no doubt at all, but at the opposite end of the arc. That was policing for you. That was following leads, asking questions and listening to answers. Listening carefully and, at the same time, assessing the reliability of the person answering. You started by 'knowing'. You ended by knowing damn-all or, at best, what you didn't want to know.

Sure there were options open. Go back home and tell Briggs to let things lie; 'Accidental Death'; leave it at that and hope for the best. Or tell the truth; murder *had* been committed, so screw as detailed a statement as possible from Foster and stand Duxbury in a dock. Okay, under hard cross-examination Foster would knacker things up and Duxbury would walk away a free man, but what then? At least Duxbury would *know*. And the talk. 'Duxbury? Oh, you mean the man charged with murdering his wife?' For the rest of his life he'd carry the no-smoke-without-fire mark against his name.

Oh sure . . . the options were there.

But not the *real* option. The option that mattered.

Harker knocked on the door and limped into the surgery. Before he seated himself in the proffered chair, he knew he had a fight on his

108

hands. Nape-Smith was one of those shorter-than-average men who carry an air of clinical purity around with them; immaculately dressed, with a whiter-than-white shirt and a tie which matched the dark blue of his suit; greying hair, with carefully combed 'wings' at each side of his head; long, white fingers with manicured nails; hard, light-blue eyes which silently dared anybody to question his diagnosis. He was a G.P, sitting at the near-obligatory roll-topped desk, surrounded by the clutter of his profession. The blood-pressure gewgaw. The glorified torch with the gadget remarkably like a cake-icing cone with which to peer into a patient's ears. The wheeled trolley in one corner, with the white cover and the nest of kidney-basins and a neatly arranged row of tweezers, scissors and probes. A tiny wall-bench, complete with bunsen burner and a wooden holder full of shining test tubes. The whole shooting match and enough terrifying paraphernalia to frighten most ill people into an immediate state of well-being.

'Beechwood telephoned,' snapped Nape-Smith. He gave a quick nod at Harker's shoes. 'Something wrong with your foot?'

Harker cleared his throat, then said, 'Yes.'

'In that case, you'd better take your . . .'

'Look, you don't want to . . .'

'Don't argue, man. I haven't X-ray eyes.'

Harker raised his voice a little, and said, 'I'm not here about my foot.'

'What?'

'That happened years ago. I'm here to ask you some questions.'

'Questions? What sort of questions?'

Harker took out his warrant card, Nape-Smith glanced at it, frowned then returned it, and waited.

'Questions about murder,' said Harker deliberately.

'Murder?' Nape-Smith glared. 'Whose murder?'

'You don't know her.'

'In that case, what the deuce . . .'

'One of the witnesses is your patient.'

'I still don't see . . .'

'Foster. Raymond Foster.'

'Foster . . . I know Foster. I still don't . . .'

'I'd like to ask you some questions about him.'

'Are you *mad*?' Nape-Smith's expression reflected outrage beyond description.

'No more than the average man,' said Harker gently.

'You're a policeman, aren't you?'

'You've seen my warrant card. Detective sergeant.'

'And you don't know about the Hippocratic Oath? Good God, you're not fit to . . .'

'Crap,' said Harker bluntly.

'What?'

'We're in the twentieth century . . . and we aren't in Greece. I handle modern English Criminal Law. All that Hippocratic Oath malarky doesn't mean a damn thing.'

'How dare you!'

'I dare,' said Harker pointedly, 'because *I* know the law. You don't.'

'The confidentiality between doctor and patient is . . .'

'As I've already said. So much crap. Like the legendary "confidentiality" between priest and penitent. Parent and child. For your information, the only relationships of confidentiality recognised by Criminal Law are those between a lawyer and his client, and man and wife. You're not a lawyer . . . and you're not married to Raymond Foster. You have a straight choice. You answer the questions now. Here, in the privacy of this surgery, or when the case comes to court I slap a subpoena in your lap and you answer them in open court, in the front of eager little newspaper reporters . . . or risk being sent down for contempt of court. Make the decision, doctor. Now. You may be red hot at dishing out pills and potions, but when it comes to law don't start telling me *my* job.'

'I – I won't . . .'

'You *will*.'

'Look, Beechwood didn't say anything about . . .'

'I know what Beechwood said. I was alongside him at the time. This is a crime enquiry, doctor. A *murder* enquiry. Keep that in mind before you start hiding behind mythical oaths and confidentialities.'

It was a gamble, and Harker knew it was a gamble. He was using the law – valid and quite genuine law – for his own ends. The bluff was that no prosecution would dream of calling evidence in order to bolster the credibility of another witness. Indeed, it was doubtful whether a Crown Court would allow such evidence, but that was something Nape-Smith *didn't* know. Thus the bluff, plus a certain amount of practical psychology. This pompous little medic wasn't used to being bounced back from a brick wall; in his own eyes he was a minor god and not being treated as such knocked him off balance. For the moment Harker had him in the palm of his hand.

Nape-Smith croaked, 'Who's the fool murdered?'

'Foster? Nobody. But he *witnessed* a murder.'

'Oh!'

'He's our main witness. He'll be cross-examined. What we don't want is some barrister to make mincemeat of him.'

'That wouldn't be too difficult,' muttered Nape-Smith.

'That's my own impression. I want to know the reason.'

'He's unstable,' said Nape-Smith. Some of his authority was returning, and he spoke without hesitation. 'Some people *are*.'

'Not mad.' Harker's tone carried a hint of warning. 'Not round the twist. He's a physics master. He knows his subject. He can *think*.'

'We have a term for it. The psychiatrists . . .'

'Psychiatrists!'

'. . . call it Panphobia. A fear of most things. Of almost everything.'

'Balls,' said Harker very deliberately.

'Look, if you're not prepared to . . .'

'He's a schoolmaster. He stands in front of a class. I'm told he can interest that class in certain subjects. He goes out and about. I have it on good authority that he is capable of expressing his opinions to complete strangers. He's been called unsure of himself. Unable to exert discipline. That sort of thing. I've met him. I've talked to him. My own impression for what it's worth. He's a walking contradiction.'

'For what it's worth,' echoed Nape-Smith.

'Fear doesn't come into it,' insisted Harker. 'Timidity – timidity in things he's not used to . . . but not *fear*.'

'If you know him . . .' began Nape-Smith.

'I don't *know* him. I've merely *met* him. Talked with him.'

111

'He's just had a breakdown . . .'

'I know that, too.'

'He's perpetually on the brink of a breakdown. He'll have others.'

'Haven't you some say in that?' asked Harker brusquely.

'I prescribe pills. I presume he takes them. I can only assume he'd be worse than he is without them.'

'And that satisfies you?'

'Sergeant, I'm not a miracle-worker. I'm a doctor. Whatever you think – of me or of doctors in general – I consider myself a good doctor. But there are things I can't alter. Things nobody can alter – the personality of a fellow human being.'

Harker nodded, as if half-convinced, then growled, 'He's our main witness. If he's weak, a murderer walks away a free man.'

Nape-Smith drummed the surface of his desk, softly, with the tips of the fingers of one hand, and waited.

'Dope,' said Harker softly.

'By that you mean drugs?'

'The official name.'

'I prescribe them. Those I think he needs.'

'I'm talking about the hard stuff.' Harker's tone was harsh with urgency. 'Something to give him backbone. Temporarily. Something he can take before he goes into a witness box. Something to make him equal to any cross-examination in the world.'

'You're mad.' Nape-Smith looked shocked. Nor was it play-acting.

'Are there such drugs?' insisted Harker.

'I wouldn't prescribe them.'

'*Are* there?'

'Yes.' Nape-Smith nodded. Pomposity had been replaced by a quiet, simmering rage. 'Injections. Capsules. They're available at mental institutions. They're *not* available over a chemist's counter.'

'Can you prescribe them?'

'If I could, I wouldn't.'

'A murderer walks free. Doesn't that . . .'

'Look! That's *your* problem. My duty is to my patient. And,' he continued before Harker could interrupt, 'don't start quoting the

112

law to me. That I *do* know. I'd risk being struck off the Medical Register if I pumped that stuff into him. I won't even tell you their names. Not even that.'

'Don't you care that . . .'

'No. Frankly, I don't give a damn. There is nothing – no argument you can use – to force me to scramble Foster's brain for your benefit. That's what would happen. Short of a miracle, that's what *must* happen. We're talking about the human brain, man. A very delicate piece of mechanism. And you have the blind audacity to suggest that, figuratively speaking, I hit it with a sledge-hammer. That I tip the finely balanced sanity of an innocent man, in order that you can win a court case.'

Very solemnly, Harker said, 'I have your word? You're not exaggerating?'

'I am not exaggerating, sergeant.' Having made his point, Nape-Smith quietened a little. 'This muck – this hell's brew the chemical scientists create – it has its uses. Desperate diseases . . . that sort of thing. But it's not for the man-in-the-street and it's not for the ordinary G.P. It creates madness. A form of madness. The wrong dosage – *any* dosage, without strictly controlled clinical tests – and, you'd have your fearless witness. Oh, yes. You'd also have a potential psychopath. A creature capable of more than one murder. And it isn't possible to talk about a "temporary basis". How long would it last? I don't know. Nobody knows with absolute certainty. Sometimes forever.' Then in a near-pleading tone. 'Don't pursue this line, sergeant. You have my solemn assurance, you'll regret it. Whatever else he is, Foster isn't an evil man. Don't make him one. Not for the sake of a conviction . . . not even for a conviction for murder.'

'It wouldn't have worked.' Harker's shoulders sagged a little. His voice carried a near-acceptance of defeat. 'Damnation, it was just an idea. A thought. It would still have been one man's word against another's. However tough. Whatever sort of a witness.' He looked into the medic's eyes and, suddenly, there was a rapport between them. 'Thanks for letting me waste your time, doctor. Let's say, I had to know. Had to be sure.'

'I'm sorry.' There was genuine regret in the words. They both stood up and, as they shook hands, Nape-Smith said, 'I know how

113

you must feel. A terminal disease . . . and I'm helpless. Some professions include burdens almost too heavy to carry.'

'Something like that,' sighed Harker. 'Something very much like that.'

Nape-Smith had talked about 'the man-in-the-street'. He'd talked about 'burdens almost too heavy to carry'.

Harry Harker lay in bed in the four-star hotel and, instead of sleep, those phrases played ring o' roses in his mind. That and first impressions. His first impression of Nape-Smith, for example. It had been wrong. Monstrously wrong. Here was a medic who, despite outward appearances, cared. Forget that first brusque, sergeant-major tone. Remember that a conscientious G.P. is a man, himself under stress. The skivers. The hypochondriacs. The idiots who dash to a doctor at the slightest sniffle. And, of course, the unfortunates with terminal disease. That, plus working all hours and the resultant loss of sleep.

Much like coppers. Good coppers who take their job seriously. The wheat and the chaff. The sheep and the goats. In both jobs, fallible men were expected to make infallible decisions. Ask – demand – the impossible . . . and the poor bastard at the receiving end suffered.

Harry Harker. Himself a strange man. Oh, a fine copper – a fine detective – with all the qualities that implied. A refusal to be licked. A refusal to be compromised. A determination well beyond the determination of most men. The son of a country vet, he lived in the cottage where he'd been born; where he'd seen first his father, then his mother, die. No sisters. No brothers. No aunts, no uncles, therefore no cousins. He'd never married. At first he'd been too shy. Thereafter he'd been too busy. Lots of acquaintances – people with whom he happily passed the time of day – but no friends. Yet never lonely. The job, his books, his record collection. He hadn't *time* to be lonely. Many men – most men – would have been miserable living such a life. Most men were herd animals but, just occasionally, a loner was thrown up. A loner who needed nobody to complete his life. And let that loner be a stalker – a man-hunter – and the result was . . . Harry Harker.

114

PART FIVE

The Diary of John Duxbury

This morning I went to church. I prayed. I prayed for Maude's soul. Prayed that it might have the peace it deserves. Basically, she was a good woman. I think she tried to understand. Tried not to be so biased about certain things. She loved me. Of that I'm certain. She wasn't demonstrative, but nevertheless she loved me.

I also prayed for myself. Prayed for strength. I need strength – great strength – to live through the next few months. Through Christmas. It will be a frightful Christmas. It *must* be. Without Maude. Without her laughter. And after . . .

Everybody insists that time heals all wounds. I wonder. At this moment, I doubt it. I doubt whether I will ever feel true happiness again. Without Maude life is empty. Meaningless. All I've lived for, all I've worked for – all we've both worked for – reduced to nothing.

This empty house. So cold. So dead. Even the world outside. Cold and dead, as if in mourning for her. As if sharing my sadness.

Don't blame yourself, Harry. I know the suggestion of our taking a short holiday was originally your idea, but don't blame yourself. I agreed. It seemed such a good idea at the time. Such a fine idea. She enjoyed herself. Her last day alive, she laughed and was happy. Remember only that. Forget the accident. Forget the fall. Only that it was quick. Not lingering, like some foul disease. She loved you. She loved us both. And it was quick and without pain. Be like me. Grasp what little comfort you can from that small mercy.

The firm is yours now. I doubt whether I shall ever be able to bring myself to . . .

PART SIX

The Agony of Raymond Foster

Martha Foster watched her husband and wondered what she could do to help. Love. Her kind believed passionately in the power of love. Universal love, the all-embracing love for every fellow-man, the love of all creatures on earth and, as far as she and Raymond were concerned, their love for each other. No qualifications. No tiny corners where that love couldn't reach. Love . . . period.

To see suffering was to suffer. To see pain was to feel pain. To witness death was to die a little. Hurt – hurt of any kind – was the only evil in the world. Remove all hurt and Eden would be re-created.

She slowly reached out a hand and clasped the fingers around his clenched fist.

'My dear,' she said gently, 'it had to be done.'

'No!' The mental agony constricted his throat and made his voice hoarse. 'I shouldn't have told. I haven't the right.'

'He killed his wife,' she insisted.

He repeated in a softer, harsher tone, 'I haven't the right.'

'A duty,' she murmured.

'I'm not God. It won't give her life. He'll suffer. We all have consciences. He'll suffer. Who am I to add to that suffering?'

'Think of *her*,' she urged.

'No, think of *him*. Locked away, like an animal. Part of his life taken from him. That, on top of what he must already be feeling. And my fault. Because I was weak. Because I couldn't resist the conventions of what we call "civilisation". If I could only . . .'

He choked into silence, and her hand tightened around his fist.

They'd walked from the hotel. Inland and away from the cliffs.

121

They'd found a tree-lined path – part of a Forestry Commission plantation – and, well into the wood, a tiny picnic area, complete with rough-hewn benches and log-topped tables. Deserted in mid-December it had invited them to rest, and they'd accepted the invitation. It was cool, dim and smelled of the pines which surrounded them. And Foster had placed his forearms on the table, clenched his fists and silently agonised at a decision he wished he hadn't made.

A thousand people taken at random would not have understood, but his wife understood. There'd been a choice. A choice of evils. To allow a fellow-creature to be murdered, and say nothing; a quick death with, hopefully, little or no pain. That, or send a fellow-creature to a cage; to a slower and infinitely more degrading death. For it *was* going to be death. Duxbury was not a young man, nor yet a fit man. A rich man used to the luxuries of life. Pampered and cosseted. He couldn't possibly live through twenty years – even ten years – of prison life.

He raised his head and peered into the gloom of the surrounding pine forest.

'Why prisons?' he groaned. 'Why *prisons?*'

'My dear, we're not able to . . .'

'They're sick. God, isn't that obvious? They're sick, not evil. No sane man kills his wife. No healthy man. He can leave her. Divorce her. Not *kill* her. That he chooses to kill her is proof enough. He needs help.' He paused. His eyes seemed to re-focus until he was gazing well beyond the confines of the trees. He continued, 'You stand in a witness box. And you try to explain this. These simple truths. And they're mad, and try to make *you* sound mad. Madmen sitting in judgement on a sick man. And they call that "justice". To understand. Just to try to *understand*, but they don't even *try.*'

'You're right, dear. Of course you're right.' She squeezed his fist, comfortingly. 'But we have to have prisons, otherwise . . .'

'Why?' He turned on her, eyes shining with fanaticism. 'It's a retrograde step. In the past – in the so called "Dark Ages" – they locked men away *pending* punishment. The *imprisonment* wasn't the punishment. The punishment was maiming or whipping . . . even hanging. But that "punishment" was all they understood. It was their idea of *treatment*. Today, we deny them treatment. The imprisonment is the "treatment". Good God, they didn't make that mistake centuries ago. They knew better than *that*.'

'Yes, dear,' she sighed.

'Why can't people *see*?' He hammered the fist onto the surface of the table. 'Why are people so blind? Lock an animal away. A dog, a cat. Anything! It turns in on itself. It goes crazy. Bars don't cure its illness. A cage can't mend a broken bone or remove a tumour. A cage *prevents* recovery. It's ill. Something's out of balance. It needs curing, not caging. Why not men? Holy Christ, why do they insist that caging a sick man can do more than caging a sick animal can do?'

'Please,' she pleaded. 'You've done nothing wrong. You *couldn't*.'

He stared at the planks of the table, and the tears spilled from his eyes and ran down his cheeks.

'I don't hate Duxbury,' he muttered. 'I don't hate *anybody*. I don't *want* to hate anybody . . . whoever they are. There's too much hatred. So much hatred, and so little understanding. I don't hate him. But that doesn't matter. What *I* want is of no importance. The community demands vengeance. They force me to do hateful things – say hateful things – and, when I try not to, they label me as mad.'

'Darling you're not mad. The others, but not you.'

'I'm *not* mad.' He turned his head and looked at her through tear-dimmed eyes. Such pleading. Such heartbreak.

'You're not mad, darling.'

She moved her hand and placed an arm across his shoulders and, as he bent his head to her breast and sobbed, she soothed him like a mother giving assurance to a frightened child.

The passion had spent itself. They'd walked slowly back to the hotel, and now he was stretched out on top of the bed, while she read to him. She read their favourite book, Steinbeck's *Travels With Charley*. A book of beauty, a book about beauty written in beautiful prose. A book which concerned itself with nature, but also with the destruction of nature and with bigotry. They'd read it aloud – she to him, or he to her – perhaps half a dozen times, and each time with a new wonder. It was 'their' book; the down-soft comfort of magnificent phrases and descriptions upon which they could rest whenever they were greatly troubled.

She could read aloud well. With a little training, and with carefully chosen roles, she might have been a moderately successful actress. The pauses were as important as the words, and her voice rose and fell to give gentle emphasis where emphasis added to the prose of a master story-teller.

Strange that this volume, written by a man who in the 'twenties and early thirties was part of the hell-raising Bohemian set of the Left Bank, could encapsulate such genuine compasssion; could chuckle so innocently at such simple things; could capture, in words, the wonderment of nature and the thoughtless vulgarity of mankind.

She read and gradually he relaxed, and the passion and fear drained from him. Strength returned. The strength of his convictions. The innocent faith which was to him a near-religion. He was right. Right! And that the bulk of men indulged in wars and talk of wars – in vengeance and injustice – made him no less right.

PART SEVEN

The Anger of Harry Harker

Harker decided to push the enquiry a little further. Just a little further. After all, he hadn't yet clapped eyes on this Duxbury character and that (to Detective Sergeant Harker) was very necessary. 'Know Thine Enemy'. You bet! Also, have a decko at him. Win, lose or draw, know what he looks like. Tuck him away for future reference . . . you never knew.

Nor had it been a good night. Harker liked his own bed. The hell with hotel beds and hotel bedrooms. They were cold and comfortless compared with his own place. Gadgets galore, but still like sleeping in a square cave. Traffic noise outside and always some clown bawling 'Goodnight' down the corridor. Doors closing, lift-gates clanging, trolleys squeaking, Hoovers moaning. Jesus wept! A square cave in Piccadilly Circus.

As he threw the bedclothes aside and hoisted himself onto the carpet, he muttered, 'Don't put any flags out yet, Mister bloody Duxbury. There has to *be* a way.'

He showered, shaved and dressed, then made his way to the dining room for breakfast. He had to wait, no longer than usual, but in his present irritable mood it *seemed* longer than usual. For the same reason, the kippers didn't taste as fresh as they should have tasted, the tea wasn't as hot as it ought to have been and the toast and marmalade wasn't quite up to scratch.

He returned to the bedroom, packed, took the lift to the ground floor and paid his bill. Then out to the Fiesta, a weaving, honking route to the outskirts of the city after which he put his foot down and was on the way towards the target of his attentions.

Protocol demanded that he should notify the new force of his

127

presence, and the reason for his being in their area. Balanced against that was an urgency to keep Duxbury in the dark as long as possible. Harker therefore decided to skip the hurdles and go for the divisional officer, personally, a certain Chief Superintendent Tallboy.

Even Harker had heard of Tallboy, the legend who, along with Ripley, Sullivan, Blayde and Collins had in the past policed the twin cities of Bordfield and Lessford, plus the surrounding county constabulary area and had handled headline cases in both orthodox and unorthodox ways and, in so doing, written their own chapters in the history of the Police Service. Now only Tallboy remained and, when he entered his office, Harker was slightly shocked. Such a mediocre-looking man. None of the bombast he'd expected. None of the arrogance. A typical 'Harry Wharton' type; on the face of it too decent ever to be truly ruthless. And yet on closer examination the lines were there on his face; the lines of strain and a small lifetime of overwork. The hair was grey and turning white. The frame slim and wiry, with the slightly bent shoulders of a man past his prime. But the eyes were steady and piercing and the handshake was cool and firm. Yes, despite outward appearances, this one might well be a good choice to guard your back in a tight corner.

Introductions over, Harker settled in a chair and explained his visit. Tallboy listened without interruption, then said, 'Not a very enviable task.'

'You know this Duxbury, sir?' asked Harker.

'A little. He runs a printing firm – him and his son – and he's well thought of.'

'He's a murderer,' said Harker flatly.

'*After* he's been convicted.'

'No, sir.' Harker's hand tightened slightly on the curve of the walking stick handle. 'Whether or not he's convicted.'

'That's not what the textbooks say, sergeant.'

Very deliberately, Harker said, 'If half the tales are true, *you've* closed the textbook more than once.'

Tallboy remained silent and waited.

'I need to know about him,' said Harker.

'He's fairly well off. Lives in a moderately big house out of town.

On Rimstone Beat.'

'Rimstone Beat?'

'A two-man outside beat. Constables Pinter and Stone.'

'Any good?' asked Harker quietly.

'Who are we talking about, sergeant?'

'The two outside beat men. Pinter and Stone.'

Tallboy's eyes narrowed fractionally as he said, 'You're talking about constables in my division.'

Harker nodded. He'd committed himself, and he wasn't the sort of man to back-pedal.

'You don't know me,' said Tallboy in a dangerously soft tone.

'I've heard of you, sir.'

'Obviously not everything.'

'Outside beats,' said Harker calmly. 'Usually reserved for the also-rans. Men who wear the uniform, but aren't coppers.'

'Not in this division.'

'If you say so, sir.'

'I don't just "say so", Sergeant Harker. I mean it.'

'Yes, sir.'

'Pinter's good. Damn good. Stone's an older man, but he can still carry corn.'

'I'm obliged, sir.' It was as near an apology as Harker was prepared to go. He continued, 'You'll have a good sergeant. One who knows things.'

'Uniform or C.I.D.?'

'Either,' then, with a half-smile, 'I know, sir. They're *all* good sergeants.'

'You're learning.'

'Look, sir.' Harker placed his cards, face upwards on the table. 'Duxbury shoved his wife over the cliff. I've one witness . . . who's no damn good. I need information. As much information as possible. There's always one man – usually a sergeant – who knows more than most. More than even *you* know.'

'A sergeant, because *you're* a sergeant?' Tallboy raised a quizzical eyebrow.

'No, sir.' Harker was very serious. 'Using your own yardstick, to hold stripes here means you're better than a P.C. Inspectors deal with admin. They're not in the thick of things as much as they'd

129

like to be.'

'You have it all worked out,' said Tallboy a little sourly.

'I'm not new at the game, sir.'

'Right.' Tallboy reached a decision. 'Sergeant Cockburn. He's uniform and if he isn't on the streets he'll be in the front office. I'll accept "suspected murder" for the time being. See Cockburn. Tell him you've my authority. Use Pinter and Stone as you see fit.'

'Thank you, sir.'

'Just one thing.' Tallboy leaned forward slightly. 'You'll be seeing Duxbury?'

'Eventually.'

'When – if ever – you have enough to twist his tail.'

'That's the size of it, sir.'

'I want to be there.'

'Sir, I don't think . . .'

'I'm not *asking*, sergeant. This is my division. *I* want to decide whether or not I have a wife-killer on my doorstep.'

'Of course, sir.' Harker nodded his agreement. 'Thank you, sir.'

They sat in the canteen. Formica-topped tables, tubular chairs, plastic cruet sets, tin ash-trays, strip-lighting, polished composition floor and in one corner 'The Monster' . . . a hot-drinks vending machine. Harker sipped scalding noodle soup from a thin, plastic container. Cockburn, tunic unfastened, seemed to enjoy unsweetened, unmilked coffee. Harker idly wondered whether police canteens arrived packed in a standard do-it-yourself kit. They all looked the same, all smelled the same, all gave the impression of comfort but were in some odd way *un*comfortable. It was late afternoon and they had the canteen to themselves. Between sips of coffee, Cockburn smoked a cigarette. He didn't know this jack Harker, but first impressions were favourable.

He said, 'Tallboy runs a tight ship.'

'A claim they all make,' murmured Harker.

'In his case not an empty claim.'

'Makes a pleasant change.' Harker grinned. 'My gaffer doesn't know prow from starboard.'

'Hard,' sympathised Cockburn.

'John Duxbury.' Harker firmly flipped the conversation onto

his chosen rails.

'Printer.' Cockburn drew on the cigarette. 'Best printing firm in Beechwood Brook. Best for miles around. He runs it with his son, Harry.'

'As a man?' pressed Harker.

'Married. Self-made. Just the one lad. Lives out of town, Rimstead way.'

'As a *man*?' insisted Harker. He added, 'And he's not married any more. He nudged his wife off a cliff.'

Cockburn pursed his lips into a silent whistle, but didn't look shocked.

'That's why I'm here,' added Harker.

'I wouldn't have thought . . .' said Cockburn thoughtfully.

'Too nice? Too good a citizen?'

'Not enough guts,' said Cockburn bluntly.

'Just the two of them . . . that's what *he* thought.'

'Oh!'

'A quick push and it's all over.'

'Still takes guts.' Cockburn sipped the coffee. 'People fall from cliffs and live. What then?'

'Then,' growled Harker, 'we'd have a damn-sight easier case.'

'Witnesses?' asked Cockburn.

'One . . . and he's no bloody good.'

'So . . .' Cockburn moved his shoulders in a half-shrug. 'You're building up a character.'

'Something like that.'

'They say even a worm turns,' said Cockburn thoughtfully.

'Don't give me home-spun philosophy, mate. Give me something I can get my teeth into.'

'She was a bitch.' Cockburn half-turned in the chair, rested a forearm on the chair's back, tilted his head and seemed to concentrate on the ceiling. 'On the face of things, happily married. Money enough to attend the various social functions. Mayor's Ball, that sort of thing. Out front when royalty visits . . . which isn't often. Part of the town, but not *of* the town . . . if you get what I mean.'

'No, I don't,' grunted Harker.

'This place. Beechwood Brook.' Cockburn sipped coffee and

131

puffed cigarette smoke. 'Like everywhere else. Social cliques. The Freemason crowd. The Round Table crowd. Clubs. Organisations. That sort of thing. So-called "professional men". One night a week, one night a month – whatever. Charitable stunts. Get-togethers as an excuse for belting the booze. It's part of the fabric of every town. Solicitors, bank managers, accountants, proprietors of the main firms . . . managing directors maybe. Duxbury's not part of it. Twice, to my knowledge, they've wanted him to stand for the council. Once for the Magistrates' Bench. He turned 'em down.'

'Not a social animal?'

'My impression,' said Cockburn, 'is that he wouldn't have minded. Just that his missus might not have approved.'

'Most wives would be happy.'

'She wants – *wanted* – him there. There!'

'Where she could keep an eye on him?'

'About it,' agreed Cockburn.

'Women?' asked Harker with mock-innocence.

'If so, she was on a loser. We get to know most things – you will at your place – but not *that*. Not so much as a hint.' Cockburn paused, then continued, 'Although a couple of weeks back – late November – he called in at the station here. Some snivelling "private investigator" was trailing round after him. His wife was paying. Some forbidden "love nest" somewhere, but that was crap.'

'You're so sure?'

'Harker, old son, they have that *look*. And they're fidgety. Even the brazen bastards . . . and Duxbury's not that.'

'It could be the motive we're looking for,' argued Harker.

'Again . . . no guts.' Cockburn waved the cigarette in a gesture of contempt. 'He's a runt. A well-dressed runt, a well-heeled runt, a well-spoken runt . . . but still a runt. They don't come any less than him.'

'Runts can commit murder,' argued Harker doggedly.

The way of so many murder enquiries. Not the gore-soaked killings. Not the shootings or the knifings. The 'quiet' murders . . . which just might *not* be murders. Make a decision. Who to believe. Then, right or wrong, push that decision to an absolute conclusion. Put a name to the murderer, then ask questions around him. Know him, before you meet him. His character, his weaknesses, his strengths.

'Is he liked? Respected?'

'He isn't *dis*liked. Yes . . . I'd say he's respected by those who know him.'

'Those who know him?'

'He hasn't many friends. Aquaintances, but not many friends.'

Push the decision to its absolute conclusion. Be sure. One way or the other, be sure. Circle the suspect, without allowing him to know he's being circled. Construct a net of opinions – a web of answers to carefully asked questions – then choose the time. That all-important timing. The smooth talk. The verbal stroking. Then with luck – with every ounce of luck you can muster – the pounce.

'How old is he?'

'I'd say around the fifty mark. Maybe a bit older.'

'And his wife?'

'If there was an inquest . . .'

'I wasn't there. I'm groping.'

'You're groping, mate. A personal opinion . . . you're groping in the dark. You'll be damn lucky to find what you want.'

'How old was she?' repeated Harker.

'A couple or three years younger than him. Maybe more.'

'A perfect marriage?' It was a question shot with sarcasm.

'Who knows?' Cockburn grinned. 'Mine's okay, other marriages don't interest me.'

'Tallboy said you could answer some questions.'

'Ask some questions that *have* answers.'

'Certainly. Did Duxbury kill his wife?'

'That wouldn't be an answer. Only an opinion.'

'As a favour. Express the opinion.'

'No,' said Cockburn bluntly. He added, 'But that's only an opinion.'

'One of us holds a wrong opinion.'

'I'm not fireproof, mate. Never claimed to be.'

Like a clock ticking. The same tick, the same question. But not *quite* the same tick; each tick a different sliver of eternity. Each question – each answer – one more particle with which to block out an unknown man called John Duxbury. Patience. The patience of

133

true C.I.D. work. Never to tire. Never to be satisfied. Never to wholly *believe* until the truth is there in the palm of the hand, visible, naked and waiting for the fingers to close.

'You knew him?'

'He was a regular lunch-time customer until – let me see – until the beginning of November. He hasn't been in here since.'

'Care to talk to me about him?'

'Well, I hardly think it's my place to . . .'

'Talk to me about him.' Harker slid his open warrant card across the table. 'Here. In comfort.'

The manager frowned, sighed, then sat down on the chair across the table from Harker.

It had been a good meal. Nothing fancy, but nicely presented and with smiling service. The steak had been grilled expertly, the French fries had *been* French fries and not warmed-up crisps, the button mushrooms might well have come from a can, but after leaving the can they'd been properly cooked, the onion rings had been crisp and tasty with not too much fat, the string beans had been young and not soggy with water. A good meal. And now the biscuits were crumbly, the butter-pats freshly rolled, the cheese moist Wensleydale and the coffee served in a real cup (not one of those thimble-sized affairs) and it was *real* coffee with *real* cream.

Harker had enjoyed the meal and at the coffee stage had asked to speak to the manager.

The manager, a slightly stout, slightly sweaty man, dressed in appropriately conservative dress had arrived at the deliberately chosen table and murmured, 'Yes, sir?'

'You're the manager?'

'Yes, sir.'

'I'm told a certain John Duxbury used this café. Probably still uses it.'

'He's used it in the past, sir. May I know why you ask?'

'You know him?'

'He was a regular lunch-time customer until – let me see – until the beginning of November. He hasn't been in here since.'

And now the manager sat uncomfortably in the chair opposite Harker, wiped the hint of sweat from his palms onto the thighs of his trousers, and waited.

'A nice meal,' complimented Harker.

'Thank you, sir.'

'Duxbury. Why did he stop coming here?'

'I – I really don't know, sir.'

'Don't keep calling me "sir". "Sergeant" will do.'

'Yes, sir – er – sergeant.'

'What made Duxbury stop coming?'

'It's – er – it's something he can answer better than me.'

'I'm not asking him, I'm asking you.'

'I . . . couldn't say,' muttered the manager.

'How often did he use this place before – y'know . . .'

'Every lunch time. Mondays till Fridays.'

'Then he stopped. Just like that.'

'I'm afraid so.'

'Why?' Harker popped a piece of cheese into his mouth and watched the manager's face.

'I – er – I really don't . . .'

'Oh yes, you *do*.'

'I assure you, sergeant . . .'

'Why did he stop?'

'Sergeant, I don't want to say hurtful things – things I can't really substantiate – about a friend.'

'He was your friend?'

'In a way. Rather more than a customer.'

'A good enough reason for *not* stopping.'

'I – I suppose so.' The manager's tongue moistened drying lips.

'So why *did* he stop?' Harker swallowed the cheese, then added, 'You can answer the question here or I can pay my bill and leave . . . and you'll answer it somewhere else.'

'Look I . . .'

'Why did he stop being a regular customer?'

'I – I think he was embarrassed.' The words weren't far from a moan. 'He'd no need to be. It wasn't his fault.'

'Whose fault?'

'His wife's.'

'Mmm.' Harker nodded sagely. As if the manager's words had been a mere verification. Then he sipped coffee and said, 'Now,

135

let's hear *your* version of what happened.'

The manager told him. A mumbled, stammered version. Harker listened, stone-faced, as if he'd heard it all before.

'A storm in a tea-cup . . . as it were?' Harker smiled.

'She's a very difficult woman, sergeant.'

'A bitch.'

'Er – she's Mr Duxbury's wife. I can't . . .'

'Was.'

'I beg your pardon?'

'She isn't his wife any more.'

'Oh!' The manager looked startled. 'I – er – I didn't realise they were on the point of divorce.'

'It's what's known as "the thing" these days. Didn't you know?'

'Of – of course. But I never imagined *him* to be . . .'

'The divorcing kind?'

'She *was* a bitch,' breathed the manager.

'You knew *her* well, too, did you?' said Harker innocently.

'Oh, no. Just the once. When she created about the cup.'

'He told you?'

'What?'

'Duxbury. *He* told you she was a bitch?'

'Look, I don't think . . .' The manager glanced at Harker's cup. 'You've – er – finished your coffee. More?'

'Thanks.'

The manager raised a hand and a waitress came to the table and re-filled Harker's cup.

'I'll have one, too,' said the manager.

Harker waited until they were once more alone and beyond hearing distance of either the staff or the handful of other customers, then as if there had been no interruption, the slow, remorseless probing continued.

Yes, the episode about the cracked cup had been very upsetting.

No, he hadn't seen Duxbury's wife before that episode.

Yes, Duxbury was a very quiet gentleman, and very polite.

'Shy, would you say?'

'Yes, I think "shy" describes him perfectly.'

'Secretive?' pushed Harker.

'No. That would be going too far.'

'But shy?'

'Yes, very shy.'

That extra word 'very' was pounced upon. What (in the manager's opinion) was the difference between being 'very shy' and being 'secretive'? Surely it was a matter of behaviour. What sort of behaviour? Well, hiding things, that was being secretive. Not *saying* things, wasn't that also being secretive? It could be, but Duxbury had never given the impression of deliberately not *saying* anything.

'So you talked?'

'Yes.' The manager sipped his coffee. 'When I'd time – when the café wasn't too crowded – I'd call at his table for a friendly chat.'

'What about?'

'Oh . . . anything, really.'

'Specifically,' insisted Harker.

'Look.' The manager plucked a paper napkin from a holder on the table. He dabbed his lips. 'Look, sergeant. I – I feel I must ask you. These questions. There's a reason behind them, surely?'

Harker nodded and moved the spoon gently in his coffee.

'I'd like to know what that reason is.'

'No.' Harker's voice was soft, but firm. 'I know about this place. I know Duxbury lunched here. How do I know? We don't work that way. The who, the what, the how. That's something we keep to ourselves. What I've learned here – what I'll *learn* here – that's *my* business. Nobody's told. No names are mentioned.'

'Yes, but . . . the *reason?*'

'Routine enquiries.' The expression and the tone gave nothing away. 'Detailed enquiries. Beyond that I'm not prepared to say.'

'Oh!'

'What did you talk about?'

'Oh, y'know, the weather.'

'Oh, come on. Other things too.'

'The – the news. Sometimes television programmes. Photography.'

'Photography?'

'I'm a keen amateur photographer. He's interested.'

'His hobby?'

'Yes. Mine, too.'

137

'Did you swop photographs?'

'Well, no. I concentrate on landscapes.'

'And Duxbury concentrates on . . . what?'

'Portraiture.'

'Portraiture?'

'Photographs of people. Of . . .'

'I know what the word means. What kind of portraits?'

'Just – *people* . . . I suppose.'

'Strangers?'

'That was the impression.'

'Candid camera stuff?'

'I – I think so. Some of the best photographers . . .'

'Ah, but he isn't, is he?'

'What?'

'He's an amateur. Like you. He's not one of those "best photographers" you're talking about. He didn't walk around with a camera dangling from his neck . . . or did he?'

'Well, no. I've never seen his camera.'

'But you talked "photography"?'

'Yes.' The manager nodded.

'Did he know his stuff?'

'Oh, yes. Especially lighting. Back-lighting. Indirect lighting. Ways of emphasising shadows. That sort of thing.'

'Exposure time?'

'I suppose so. That's taken for granted. Anybody seriously interested in photography . . .'

'Did he show you any?'

'What?'

'Any of his photographs?'

'No.' The manager smiled and added, 'We don't, sergeant. At least, hardly ever.'

'What?'

'I'm not talking about snapshots, sergeant. We tend to look upon it as an art form. Filters. Developing time. The composition. And only about one in ten come up to expectation. We set ourselves a very high standard. Those we like – our successes – we mount and treasure. We usually destroy the failures. What we *don't* do is carry our work about in our wallets, ready to show to people.

138

Any more than serious stamp-collectors or coin-collectors do.'

Harker grunted reluctant understanding, then said, 'Right . . . you talked about photography. What else?'

'I've already . . .'

'His wife?'

'No. There was no reason to . . .'

'Married men usually mention their wives. Eventually.'

'In – er – in passing,' agreed the manager, without enthusiasm.

'Duxbury did. He *must* have.'

'In passing,' repeated the manager.

'Fine. What did he say . . . in passing.'

'Not much, really. I gather her name was Maude.'

'Maude,' agreed Harker. 'From hints – from his tone of voice – what conclusions?'

'That . . .' The manager moved a hand. 'Domineering, I suppose.' Then, hurriedly, 'But that might be wisdom after the event. After the tea cup fiasco.'

'Forget the tea cup business.'

'I'm trying to. I'm trying to be fair.'

'Did he praise her?'

'I – er – I really can't remember.'

Harker had placed his spoon in his saucer. He picked it up slowly, and began tapping the table with it. Gentle taps, with the paced rhythm of a soft heart-beat. Menacing. Almost threatening. His voice, too, changed. A subtle change. A hint that the small-talk had finished. Brittle as broken glass . . . and as dangerous.

'Maude,' he said quietly. 'Not "the wife". Not "my wife". None of the accepted ways of a long-married man mentioning his wife – as you put it – "in passing". You haven't been giving me answers, friend. All you've been doing, so far, is dodging the questions. Start answering. I want to know all *you* know about John Duxbury and Maude Duxbury.' The spoon tapped the table, and he added, 'We start from now.'

Harker booked in at a moderately good hotel. He booked in late after the receptionist had gone off duty, therefore there was only the night porter around to see to his wants. Nor was the night porter the brightest man in Beechwood Brook.

Having shown Harker to his room and turned on the central heating radiator, the night porter hesitated at the door, expectantly.

'I'd like a good, stiff drink,' said Harker.

'I don't know about that, sir.' The night porter had adenoidal trouble; the impression was that his voice was having to force itself through several layers of blotting-paper.

'What's that supposed to mean?'

'The bar's closed, sir. It's been closed more than an hour. They've all gone home.'

'I've just booked in. I'm staying the night. I'm a resident.'

'Oh, aye. But the bar's closed, and they've all gone home.'

'Haven't *you* a key to the bar?'

'No, sir.'

'I want a double whisky,' said Harker harshly. 'I've been working my nuts off. I want a nightcap . . . a double whisky.'

'They've all gone . . .'

'Has the manager gone home?'

'No, sir. He lives here.'

'Get him.'

'He won't like being disturbed.'

'For Christ's sake!' exploded Harker 'This place isn't run for *his* bloody benefit. Either get me a double whisky or get me the manager . . . just decide which.'

Harker got his double whisky.

As the night porter delivered it, Harker growled, 'Sunshine, just be warned. People who come here know the rules of the game. There's *always* basic booze available for residents. The law demands it. I know, you expected a back-hander. With a back-hander, there'd have been no argument. Well, *I* don't get back-handers so, as far as I'm concerned, *you* don't get back-handers. What you *do* get is the grandfather and grandmother of all ballockings if I ring the bell before you go off duty, and you aren't here before the echo dies away.'

The night porter left in a hurry.

Harker flopped into a chair, sipped at the whisky and had the grace to feel something of a heel. He'd vented his fury on a dopey sod who couldn't answer back . . . and that wasn't like Harker.

But, hell, this enquiry was developing into something of a one-man crusade. That restaurant manager! He'd just about pumped him dry – just about had him in tears – and for what? Duxbury had hinted, and more than hinted, that he wasn't happily married. So what *was* "happily married"? Never having been married, and having no intention of becoming married, Harker had no scale of reference. *Why* wasn't he happily married? The manager didn't know but – y'know – he thought it might be something about the sex thing. What in hell's name did that mean? Was Duxbury a poofter, or something? Good heavens, no. No suggestion of that. The – er – y'know . . . the frigid thing.

Harker sipped more whisky, blew out his cheeks in disgust and almost groaned aloud.

The lunatic had answered questions at last. But the answers had added up to damn-all. A man doesn't push his wife over the edge of a cliff because she's gone frigid on him. Not at *their* age. Otherwise the whole bloody coastline would be littered with middle-aged women with broken necks. So what was this 'sex thing' the manager had rabbited on about.

'Y'mean he's having it off with some other woman?'

'Oh, no!' The manager had looked honestly shocked at the idea. 'No. He wouldn't do *that*.'

'If he is, and his wife tumbled . . .'

'No, sir. I swear. I'd lay my life on it. Not *that*.'

'He could be having it off with *you*.'

'What?'

'If he's a queer.'

'Look! I'm not here to be insulted. You've no right . . .'

'You're here to answer questions, laddie. I'm here to *ask* them. What you're pleased to call this "sex thing". Let's be a little more specific. A *lot* more specific. Use naughty words . . . I won't mind.'

Nothing!

A lot of crappy hints, and make up your own mind. Maybe *she'd* been bouncing around on spring-interiors. Maybe *that*. If so, that was a good enough reason for doing her in. It had been in the past . . . a thousand times.

Funny, but that didn't jell. *Why* it didn't jell Harker couldn't explain. Just that it didn't. It should have – it was the easiest solution of all – but it just *didn't*.

Harker placed the whisky on a side-table and began to undress, prior to a bath.

'He *must* be a bloody homo,' he grunted.

PART EIGHT

The Quandary of James Briggs

It was a few minutes to midnight and (for him) Detective Chief Inspector James Briggs had had a hard day. A morning motoring around the various sections, checking crime stats and trends; making suggestions he knew damn well would be ignored before his car turned the first bend in the road; uttering empty pep-phrases to detective sergeants and detective constables who figured him the biggest onion ever to come from the soil; lighting mock-squibs, with as much gunpowder in them as an empty Smartie tube. In short, generally making a clown of himself . . . and knowing it.

Then paperwork. Paperwork! Hell's teeth, crime files grew thicker by the hour. Piffling little break-ins, and the forms and reports – the statements and descriptions – were like so many re-writes of *Gone With the Wind*.

Then a snatched meal and a Senior Officers' Conference. Sweating bricks to make sure he said 'Yes' and 'No' in all the right places. That bloody chief superintendent, sitting there like King Tut, thinking up every awkward question he could cull from his twisted mind. Then the quiet, sardonic, 'Not quite good enough, I think you'll agree, Chief Inspector Briggs.' No harm wished, of course, but if the bastard dropped dead while shaving tomorrow morning he (Briggs) would happily contribute to a wreath.

Then this evening. The Townswomen's Guild, and the talk he'd been conned into giving. *How To Handle A Would-be Rapist*. Judas Christ! Every last one of them as safe as a block of houses. How the hell could an aspiring rapist get going when his victim's enclosed inside a very expensive motor car? What self-respecting ravisher would give any of *them* a second glance? But they'd loved it. Lapped

145

it up. Demanded every last detail. Ah, well, maybe he was stirring a few long lost memories.

All that, plus this other thing.

Pauline Briggs floated into the room, and murmured, 'Aren't you tired, darling?'

She wore an ankle-length, pale pink dressing-gown made of heavy silk, tied with a cord of the same material. The sort of dressing-gown favoured by Hollywood beauties when Hollywood was enjoying its hey-day as a dream machine. Briggs glanced up and, for a moment, a naughty thought entered his mind. That this wife of his was that sort of a woman. A 'dream-factory' woman. As daft – as out of touch with reality – as that. She posed by the half-open door and waited for his reply.

'I'm tired,' he grunted.

'In that case, why not come to . . .'

'I couldn't sleep.' He answered the question before it was completed.

'Oh, dear.' She closed the door and glided gracefully into the room. 'Are you ill?'

'Not ill. Sick . . . sickened, really.'

'A head cold?' She folded herself elegantly into the armchair across the sheepskin hearthrug from his. 'Take an aspirin and a hot toddy.'

The drawling, third-class public school vowels grated on his nerves. God, was it worth it? Had it ever been worth it? She'd been born in Lincolnshire while her father was still a sergeant. He'd reached Briggs's own rank (chief inspector) and God only knew what sacrifices he'd made to send her to a toffee-nosed, all-girls school. Big deal! She now figured money grew on trees, that all tea was called Earl Grey and that non-tinted, non-scented writing paper was only for 'common' people.

But she was the daughter of the A.C.C, and she was *his* wife.

'It's not a head cold,' he muttered. 'I'm not ill.'

'Is – er – is something wrong?'

'Yeah.' He nodded. 'You could say something's wrong.'

'What?'

'Basically . . .' He sighed. 'Basically, I wish I wasn't a copper.'

'Don't be silly, darling. A few years and you'll be an assistant

146

chief constable, somewhere. Like daddy.'

'Like daddy,' he muttered.

'I beg your pardon?' Coolness entered her tone, as it always did whenever anybody made even token criticism of 'daddy'.

'I wish . . .' Briggs dropped his head wearily, and combed his fingers through his hair. 'I wish I knew where the hell Harry Harker is at this moment.'

'Harker?' She frowned lady-like confusion. 'Detective Sergeant Harker?'

'I'm sitting on a bomb.' He closed his eyes as if in quick prayer, opened them, then added, 'If your father ever finds out, he'll have my tripes boiled and served up on a plate.'

'What have you done *this* time?' she demanded accusingly.

'It's about that woman Duxbury. Maude Duxbury,' he confessed heavily.

'The one who fell from the cliff?'

'That's just it.' Again he ran his fingers through his hair. 'Maybe she did. Maybe she was pushed.'

'But as I recall there was an inquest. It was in the local newspaper. The verdict was . . .'

'Coroners aren't infallible . . . they only *think* they are.'

'But surely, if . . .'

'The lunatic who claims he saw him push her . . .'

' "Him"?'

'Her husband.'

'In that case . . .'

'The berk didn't report seeing it until the Tuesday. After the inquest. After the verdict.'

'Nevertheless . . .'

'And he's a lousy witness. He *could* be wrong.'

Pauline Briggs chewed a corner of her lower lip, and allowed the jigsaw pieces to fall into place. She was spoiled – all her life she'd been carefully sheltered from the less pleasant aspects of existence – but in her own feather-brained way she knew the workings of a police force. Knew that the number of guilty men walking free far outnumbered the innocent men behind bars. The system was savagely tilted against conviction. Rightly so? Perhaps. All the legal-eagles seemed to think so. It tended to make daddy's blood pressure rise, but in fairness he *was* biased. He'd worked himself old before his time and, so often, a scoundrel had stepped from the dock a free man. And now James was worrying himself into a state. And (as far as she could see) without reason.

'You've done something silly,' she said at last.

'Could be,' agreed Briggs.

'How? Why? You have a suspected murder on your hands. All you have to do . . .'

'Have I?' The question was harsh.

'What?'

'A suspected murder on my hands?'

'You've just said, somebody saw . . .'

'Somebody *says* he saw,' he corrected her. 'And he didn't say it until after the inquest. At the moment it's recorded as a simple Sudden Death. No more suspicious than a fatal road accident.'

'You must be mad!' She stared at him in disbelief.

'Pauline, my pet,' he sighed. 'I don't have your father's rank. I don't have his experience . . . not by a country mile. But one thing I *do* know. Only comparatively recently – within the last few years – has it been established that a coroner *doesn't* carry more clout than a high court judge. They're about level-pegging. That's what it boils down to. Coroners, when they get their knife in, can carve your liver out . . . and if a simple copper like me starts trying to overturn their verdict the knife goes in up to the hilt. So the verdict stays. "Accidental Death". It stays until I have more than one shaky witness to fall back on. That's what Harker's doing.'

'Harker?'

'I gave him what, I suppose, can be called a roving commission. Out of this police area. Anywhere. Just to find out whether it *was* or *wasn't* murder. I don't know where the hell he is. I don't know what the hell he's doing. The only thing I know for certain is that he has my future – *our* future – in the palm of his hand.'

'Oh, God!' she breathed.

'I don't think he dislikes me,' mused Briggs slowly. 'Or if he *does*, not actively.'

'Why – why should he?' she asked in a stumbling voice.

'What?'

'Dislike you? Why should *anybody* dislike you? You're not . . .'

148

'Wouldn't you?' he countered, bitterly.

'I don't know what you mean.'

'Chief Inspector – *Detective* Chief Inspector – Briggs . . . courtesy of "daddy".'

'You've no right to . . .'

'Oh for God's sake!' He made a swatting motion with his hand, and the worry switched to anger. 'How many men did I leap-frog? I shouldn't hold this rank. I haven't the experience, I haven't the ability, I haven't even the *age*. I'm what I am because of *who* I am. The assistant chief's son-in-law. Because of *you*. If I'd married anybody else, I'd still be working a three-shift system pounding beats. I know it. Everybody knows it. The damn chief superintendent knows it *and* resents it . . . and who can blame him? They all resent it. Dammit, *I'd* resent it in their shoes. Christ, I sit in that office sometimes and I could throw up. Nepotism gone mad.' The surge of anger quietened and in a hoarse voice he ended, 'It's not what it's about. It *shouldn't* be what it's about.'

Her eyes sparkled with held-back tears as she breathed, 'I – I didn't think you felt so strongly about it.'

'Yeah.' The anger had left him. Only self-disgust remained. 'I've lived with it till now. Till this cropped up. Now . . . God knows!'

Very tentatively she said, 'Should I have a word with . . .'

'No!' The single word was harsh and final. He took a deep breath, then in a steadier voice said, 'If we sink, we sink. No paternal life-belt . . . thank you very much. But if I ride this out . . .'

He didn't end the sentence.

She said, 'Yes, dear. I understand.'

And she almost did.

149

PART NINE

The Craft of Wilf Pinter

Police Constable 1404 Wilfred Pinter shared Rimstone Beat with P.C. Stone. It worked well. It was a vast improvement on the sorry state of affairs when Karn had shared the beat with Pinter.* Karn had been a pain in the neck. Idle. An artist at dodging both work and responsibility and, when he'd been booted out of the force and replaced by Sammy Stone, Wilf Pinter hadn't wept any tears. Stone was an older man who'd been 'put out to grass' for the final years of a typical, hard-working career. No tearer-down of temples. No breaker of dams. But a plodding guy who knew his job and did his share. Pinter was satisfied.

Wilf Pinter. A man married to his job, because these days he could think of nothing and nobody else *worth* being married to. His wife, Hannah, was dead. Like yesterday. It would always be like yesterday. All this 'time heels wounds' crap . . . crap! Those last few days, with him (Pinter) and Hannah's mother. Waiting. Praying. Knowing she was dying, not wanting her to die but, if she had to die, for her to die quickly and with as little pain as possible. And after the death of his wife? Two heartbroken, lonely people. A mother and a husband. A widow and a widower. Hannah's mother had treated Wilf like her own son and, to Wilf, the in-law part wasn't there. She'd lived at the house throughout the last stage of Hannah's illness, and when Hannah had died she'd stayed on. A good woman, repaying Pinter for the limitless love he'd given her daughter. More than a housekeeper. A substitute mother. There'd been no need to make the decision . . . it had been the natural thing to do. For both of them.

All on a Summer's Day by John Wainwright, Macmillan, 1981.

The experience had aged Pinter. He looked ten years older than his true age. He rarely smiled. His politeness was a cool, aloof politeness which kept people at arm's-length. Nevertheless, the trauma had honed him into a very special kind of policeman. Dedicated, in that he had no other interests in life. He was a copper . . . period. Other than when he slept, he kept his thoughts strictly on the job of bobbying Rimstone Beat. In effect, he was never off duty other than when he slept. In or out of uniform he forced his mind to concentrate upon those few square miles for which he and Sammy Stone were responsible. It was a trick. A gimmick. It kept his mind occupied and – as he'd learned – the mind can concentrate upon one thing only. Let it be on Rimstone Beat. Let it *never* be on Hannah.

Tallboy had telephoned the day before.

Knowing his man, Tallboy had merely said, 'There's a Detective Sergeant Harker likely to contact you. He wants to know as much as you can tell him about Duxbury.'

And Pinter had said, 'Yes, sir,' and gone about his task.

The vicar. What looked like a chance meeting. Enquiries about forthcoming Christmas plans for the church. A quiet stroll into the church and an admiration of the bits and pieces the cleric was most proud of. Questions about the possible size of the Christmas congregation compared with the size of the usual congregation. The regulars, and those who attended only at Christmas, Easter and Harvest Thanksgiving. A mild discussion concerning burial and/or cremation. A mention of the latest villager to die. Maude Duxbury. A regular church-goer? Both of them? How was he taking his loss?

Dozens of quietly spoken questions. Seemingly without pattern, but in reality, like a game of tag. The old trick of a handful of beans hidden in a barrel of beans.

A hint at the personalities of John and Maude Duxbury, as viewed from a man who had been taught to think only the best of people.

A call at the local post office-cum-general store. Were *they* ready for the Christmas rush? What extra luxuries had they been asked to get in? The off-licence side; that must be doing a roaring trade. It must be hell working out the VAT incomings and outgoings for the

154

Christmas period. It must be bad enough at *any* period. How on earth the small businesses, not large enough to employ a full-time accountant, managed was a miracle. Like Duxbury's business, for example. Duxbury had money, but money brought responsibilities, and some of those responsibilities off-set the advantages.

Again like an expert skater. Skimming the ice in apparent patternless figures, but in reality asking oblique questions which were forgotten almost as soon as they were answered.

The local medic on his rounds. They'd become more than mere doctor and patient as a result of Hannah's illness and death. When they met, they passed the time of day. What more natural, then, than to enquire how Duxbury was taking the death of his wife?

The publicans at the two nearest boozers. No direct questions. Not even oblique questions. Merely a chat and an exchange of gossip, and the main topic of gossip was Maude Duxbury's fall from the cliff. The fall, and opinions and memories of both John and Maude Duxbury. The customers had talked. The landlords had listened. Pinter played the innocent and, publicans being what they are, it had been rather like holding a bowl beneath a dripping tap. As easy as that.

That had been yesterday.

Today Pinter concentrated upon people nearer to the Duxburys. The woman who visited the house every day to clean. A great one for talking and sharing secrets. 'Not that I'm saying she was a bad woman, mind you. God rest her soul. But she didn't know the first thing about housework.' An expression of mild surprise. Even a suggestion of disbelief. 'I have a key, y'know. I let myself in. Eight o'clock. She was never out of bed before nine. Sometimes nearer ten.' A mild suggestion that the Duxburys had kept late hours; that he (Pinter) had seen lights in the house well after midnight. 'Not her. He works late in that office of his. Sups a bit too on the quiet. A couple of times I've found him asleep in that office. "Study", I think he calls it. Y'know . . . one too many.' John Duxbury? Surely not John Duxbury? 'I know. You wouldn't think so to look at him, but it's a fact. Some sort of diary. A right long-winded affair. Keeps it in the top drawer of the desk.'

Like a 'forty-niner' hitting a seam of pure gold. Just stand back and let her talk. She was a great one for talking, especially if the listener was a man. Some women were like that. Anything in pants, and they'd natter away for hours. Just nod occasionally and fill in the blank spaces with murmured nothings. Then collect the nuggets.

That evening, Pinter strolled into one of the pubs he'd visited the day before. He ordered a pint, then ambled to the table where Duxbury's gardener always sat for his nightly glass. Just the two of them. Of a kind. Taciturn, and given to listening rather than talking.

The gardener was a stocky man. Weather-beaten and round-shouldered from his trade. Steady-eyed, given to weighing his words very carefully before speaking. Rock-steady and in no way like the gossip-mongering housekeeper.

Pinter nodded a solemn greeting and the gardener grunted and returned a half-smile.

Pinter tasted his beer, then opened the conversation with, 'Real greenhouse weather.'

'There's enough to do.'

Pinter nodded silent understanding, and allowed the silence to wrap itself around them for a few moments.

Then, 'Think he'll sell the house?'

'Duxbury?'

'Seems a big place for one man.'

'I reckon.'

'Unless,' contemplated Pinter, 'he plans to re-marry.'

'Bit soon for that.'

'No, I didn't mean he had somebody in mind.'

There followed more beer-sipping silence.

The gardener wiped his mouth with the back of a hand, and said, 'He might have alterations.'

'You think?'

'Just live in part of it. Let his lad have the rest.'

'Possible,' agreed Pinter.

'Can't see him getting married again.'

'Mmm.' Then Pinter lied, 'I hear he's taken it badly.'

'Shock, I reckon.'

'Must have been.'

'They were close.'

156

'Uhu.'

'Wanders about like a lost soul. Doesn't know what to do with himself.'

'As you say, it's a bit soon.'

The hum of boozer small-talk hemmed them in. Gave them a strange privacy. It rained outside and new cus omers entered, then shook the moisture from their macs like dogs emerging from a river. The gusting wind blew the rain against the windows occasionally. Soft drum-rolls of weather settling down for a bad spell.

They drank slowly. Happy enough to be in each other's company, but not wishing to interrupt things with too much talk.

The gardener said, 'He should get out a bit more.'

'Duxbury?' Pinter made it sound as if he'd momentarily forgotten the subject of their conversation.

'He wanders about the house too much.'

'He's a big enough garden.'

'Two acres.' The gardener sipped beer. 'It doesn't interest him.'

'Gardening?'

'Somewhere to have tea in summer.'

'I've seen her in the garden a few times,' volunteered Pinter.

'Cutting flowers, that's all. Neither of them interested.'

Pinter allowed a few moments of silence to pass, then observed, 'A bit of fresh air in his lungs might do good.'

'What I think.'

'In his place,' said Pinter, 'I'd use the garden. Therapy. Come for a chat with you, perhaps.'

'No.' This time the gardener allowed the silence to build up, then added, 'Nowhere without his car. People have forgotten how to use their legs.'

'Leaves it all to you?'

'He pays well. I do my best.'

'He's lucky.'

'Happen.'

The gardener fished a charred cherry-wood from his jacket pocket. The bowl was half-charged with carbonised tobacco. He sucked the flame of a match onto its black surface and blew smoke to one side of Pinter. It stank like the very devil.

157

'Home grown?' ventured Pinter.

'Better than the stuff you buy.'

'Stronger.'

'It's an acquired taste.'

For perhaps another half hour they sat with each other. Silence, punctuated with short observations concerning the weather, the coming Christmas, inner-city hooliganism . . . not another mention of the Duxburys. Then Pinter drained his glass and stood up.

'That's my quota,' he said.

'Aye.' The gardener nodded.

'I'll wish you goodnight.'

'Goodnight.'

Later, when he was in uniform and driving his Panda van around the sleeping villages which went to make up Rimstone Beat, Pinter allowed his mind to assess and reach half-conclusions.

Why the Duxburys? Why John Duxbury? Tallboy hadn't said . . . just that this detective sergeant would be in touch. But why the *Duxburys*?

A nice enough couple. Monied, but they didn't flash it around. They'd kept themselves to themselves. Was that bad? The cleaning woman? Discount much of what *she'd* said. A village gossip who automatically spiced everything up as much as possible.

John Duxbury? Acting a little strange. God, he (Pinter) had 'acted a little strange' after the death of Hannah. Part of the price you pay for being happily married. That wasn't suspicious. Not even unusual. He'd get over it. Not completely, perhaps, but in part. Okay, chances were he wouldn't marry again. What of it? He (Pinter) wouldn't marry again. No way! Get people close enough, and it was almost a form of adultery. Pick the right one. That was it. You were lucky. Very lucky. There was never *two* right ones. Life wasn't that kind.

So, why the hell Duxbury?

PART TEN

The Frustration of Harry Harker

Christ, what a day! Detective Sergeant Harry Harker wasn't frightened of graft. He could live on tea, fags and no sleep for three days on the trot. He'd done it before. It was part of being a jack – the part nobody mentioned – when you stowed the uniform in moth-balls and jumped up to the ears into conniving bastards and lying hounds. The big jobs – the bank jobs, the major rip-offs, the killings – you always started with leeway to make up. When the whistle blew, the villains were always one jump ahead. *They* knew which direction they were heading for. *You* had to guess, and sometimes you started by guessing wrong.

But that was okay. Part of the rules of the chase. And you had a machine behind you. A hundred men on house-to-house . . . chances were you'd get *something*. A major crime? Great. Shove a detective superintendent – maybe even a detective chief superintendent – at the head of a small army. Organise an Incident Centre. Plug into the Police Computer. Get things *done*. You'd enough men and equipment to chase up every blind alley in the world. Eventually, you'd find the alley that *wasn't* blind. You had snouts prepared to take 'blood money' in exchange for tip-offs. You had radio and telephone link-ups. Money and man-hours didn't mean a damn thing.

But this!

A murder hunt, for God's sake. One man. One piddling detective sergeant . . . and not even in his own police area. And maybe it wasn't even a murder hunt. That creep Foster. The 'George Washington' character who couldn't tell a lie. Who knew? Who the hell *could* know? Why the bloody hell couldn't he keep his damn binoculars on birds. He was supposed to be bird-watching.

161

Why didn't he *watch* birds?

Some of our policemen are, indeed, wonderful. The vast majority
are like Detective Sergeant Harker. They have their off days. They
get testy and irritable. They have doubts; massive doubts where
previously they were so sure. A feeling of helplessness engulfs
them. It saps the energy and kills the enthusiasm. 'The hell with
it,' they say. 'A crime has been committed or *might* have been
committed. What difference? Solve it. Put every piece of the puzzle
into its allotted place. Perfect. So what? There'll be another crime
waiting. Then another. Then another. Like that ancient statistic
about the Chinese marching, four abreast, past a given spot. The
march is endless. They're being born faster than they pass. Same
with crime. It's being committed faster than it can be detected. A
gag? Check with the rising crime statistics. The bastards are being
born faster than we can put 'em away.'

A strange town. Miserable weather. The craziest enquiry ever
thought up. And who the hell to question without tipping the wink
to Duxbury?

Harker parked the Fiesta and strolled past the Duxbury printing
works. Dull, grey, northern stone, rain-soaked and dripping from a
cracked gutter at one corner. A regular 'muck-and-brass' place. It
looked solid. It *looked* indestructible. The view of it did nothing to
raise Harker's spirits.

He toyed with the idea of calling everything off. Calling it a day.
Packing his suitcase and returning to his own stamping ground
and telling Briggs to stew in his own stupid juice. What the hell did
he owe Briggs? Detective chief inspector! He wouldn't even make a
good boy scout.

And yet . . .

Harmless. That was the hell of it. Having found a back-door way
to the promotion ladder, why couldn't he be a ring-tailed sod and
have done with it? Why did he have to tacitly agree that he was no
damn good? The easy way? The smart way? Was he grinning
behind his hand and taking everybody for a ride?

It was possible. It had been done in the past. 'I don't know,
please help me.' My Christ, *that* little number had been used often

162

enough by idle buggers who didn't *want* to work. And he (Harker) had been pulled by it more than once. In the old days when he'd been a flatfoot. Some multiple smash-up – a fatal road accident – and a file an inch thick, in triplicate, to be passed to the force prosecuting solicitor. Oh, yes. He'd fallen for it. A real dog's dinner shown to him by a tearful colleague. A plea for guidance. Then a complete re-type . . . by Joe Muggins.

Was he still being Joe Muggins? Still fishing red-hot chestnuts out of the fire, because somebody wouldn't learn how to use the tongs?

By God, if he *was*!

Thus, throughout that miserable day, Harker's mood fluctuated. Anger. Irritation. Self-disgust. Hopelessness. Grudging pity for Briggs. Inward fury at the weakness of Foster.

A mixture that got him nowhere. That sent him questioning people who only knew Duxbury by name, or didn't know him at all. Newsagents. Publicans. Tobacconists. He even thought of calling in at the offices of the local newspaper, but that would have been foolish. Things were hairy enough without having some nosey reporter traipsing along.

He ended up in the police canteen, spilling his worries out to a cynical Sergeant Cockburn.

'You said you could do it,' grinned Cockburn.

'I've never claimed to fold water.'

'Or knit fog.'

'That's what it boils down to.'

'Seen the lad, yet?' asked Cockburn.

'Duxbury's son?'

'He's straight.'

'As far as I can see, so's his bloody father,' snorted Harker.

'The other day you sounded very sure.'

'Aye.' This time Harker grinned, albeit a little shamefacedly. 'Call it the male menopause.'

'See young Harry Duxbury,' suggested Cockburn solemnly.

'Against his own father?'

'You're not screaming "murder!" yet.'

'True, but if murder *has* been committed.'

'It's a risk,' admitted Cockburn.

'Calculated?' Harker matched Cockburn for solemnity.

'I would,' said Cockburn.

'Nevertheless, a hell of a risk.'

Very quietly, Cockburn said, 'He's been brought up right. He's been taught to respect coppers. That's not very common these days.'

'Coppers!' Deep bitterness and disgust rode Harker's exclamation.

'You shouldn't have joined, mate.' Cockburn's rejoinder was the standard return-remark. Then in a more sympathetic tone, he added, 'Take it day at a time. The rough and the smooth. You should know that by this time.'

'My old man was a vet,' mused Harker. 'A James Herriot type. Out all weathers. Day and night. It killed him. Overwork. But he was happy. To the last. Till his body couldn't take any more and his heart gave out. But – like I say – he was happy. He'd *done* something. He hadn't spent his whole life running round in ever-decreasing circles until he ended up with his nose up his own arse. Like us. Like you and me. This used to be a good job. Safe. Respectable. The sort of job people dreamed about with a good pension at the end. Dammit, it could *still* be a good job, if we didn't have to carry so many bloody passengers. Like the useless clown who sent me on this pantomime. Like barmy chief constables who think they can stroke tigers and not get their damn-fool hands chewed off.'

'You've got it bad,' observed Cockburn.

'I've had a gutful,' admitted Harker.

'Tell you what.' Cockburn tapped the Formica top of the table with the end of a forefinger. 'I'll telephone young Duxbury. He knows me. I'll make an appointment for you to see him at the office. I won't hint at what it's about. Just that you'd like to see him . . . straighten a few things out about his mother's death. Routine stuff. Five o'clock tomorrow okay?'

'Why not?' sighed Harker.

'Fine.' Cockburn nodded confidently. 'He'll help. Guide the conversation along the right lines . . . you'll get somewhere.'

Harker decided to have an early night. By ten-thirty he was in his hotel bed with a large whisky standing ready on the bedside table.

164

On his way from the nick he'd called in at a late-evening newsagent's and bought a paperback, to read and make his eyes tired. It was an appropriate book with which to end a miserable day. A Yankee private eye yarn in which the hero alternated between unholstering his gun and unzipping his pants. Blood-soaked soft porn churned out by some idiot with an over-active imagination.

Having struggled through twenty pages, Harker tossed the book onto the bedroom carpet and growled, 'Jesus wept! He should have *my* job.'

PART ELEVEN

The Conning of Harry Duxbury

Some men give an immediate impression of honesty. It is there in the firmness of their handshake, the hint of genuine pleasure in their expression, the quiet steadiness of their voice. You know, if you are any judge of fellow-men, that meanness has no place in their personality. Nor is it play-acting; there is a natural depth of sincerity which no actor on earth can imitate.

It was there in Harry Duxbury.

He waved Harker to a comfortable, leather wing-backed chair, and said, 'Please sit down, sergeant.' Then to the secretary who had escorted Harker to the office, 'Coffee please, Joyce. And no telephone calls till Sergeant Harker leaves.

'Sergeant Cockburn telephoned.' Duxbury lowered himself into a twin of the chair occupied by Harker. 'It's very considerate of you to come to me, rather than father. He hasn't got over the shock yet.'

'Ah – er – yes.'

Harker silently congratulated Cockburn. The uniformed sergeant had cunningly unlocked a door . . . it now depended upon the skill of Harker. The door *could* be opened. Gently. Slowly. Opened wide enough to see what might be beyond.

'A few things,' began Harker. 'Trivialities the coroner would like clearing up.' He smiled. 'Coroners are queer cattle.'

'They have their job to do.' Duxbury returned the smile.

'Your mother.' Harker paused to clear his throat a little. 'Was she subject to dizzy spells? Fainting? That sort of thing?'

'No.' Duxbury shook his head slowly. He added, 'Not that I know of . . . and I'm sure it would have been mentioned.'

Harker slipped his notebook from the inside pocket of his jacket, and made brief notes with a ballpoint before continuing.

169

'When she came downstairs, did she tend to hang onto the bannisters?'

'No. In fact, she was remarkably fit for her age.'

'Recent illness?'

'No. Other than an occasional cold. Sniffles. That sort of thing.'

'Vertigo?'

'No.' Then Duxbury added, 'I suppose we all do to some extent. 'But I never heard her complain of heights, or even suggest she was frightened of them.'

The coffee arrived. The woman, Joyce, brought it into the office on a neat little table with folding legs. She placed it mid-way between the two chairs.

'Thanks,' smiled Duxbury, then to Harker, 'Help yourself, sergeant. Cream and sugar to taste. The biscuits are rather nice.'

They both leaned forward in their chairs and busied themselves pouring and stirring. The woman left. Harker thought out the next possible line of questioning, and at the same time glanced around the office. Good, solid, office furniture. Good, quietly patterned carpet. Nothing superfluous. Light and airy. The office reflected the man. Clean-looking. Honest-looking.

He leaned back in his chair and said, 'Some people . . .' He paused, then continued, 'In winter when the pavements are icy. Packed snow on the ground. Some people walk quite normally. Others. They walk very gingerly. Frightened of skidding and falling. How did your mother walk?'

'Quite normally.' Duxbury's lips curled upwards a little as he continued, 'Much more confidently than father. He – like you say – expected to slip at every step.'

'The path along the cliff edge,' said Harker. 'Have you seen it?'

'No.' Duxbury shook his head. 'Father telephoned, of course. I went straight to the hotel. That's where I stayed most of the time.'

Harker said, 'It's an ordinary footpath. Less than a yard wide. Unsurfaced. A bit muddy when it rains, and it had been raining.'

'Yes. Father said so. He said it was slippery.'

'That,' said Harker slowly, 'is one of the queries. Slippery, but not all *that* slippery.'

Duxbury waited.

Harker continued, 'Your mother was firm-footed. Your father

isn't.' He hesitated, as if embarrassed to speak the words, then said, 'Is it possible – just possible – that *he* slipped and, in trying to save himself, knocked your mother off balance?'

'It's . . . possible.' Duxbury weighed his answer carefully. He continued, 'But I don't think that's what happened.'

Harker raised questioning eyebrows.

Duxbury said, 'He gave evidence at the inquest. I don't think he'd lie under oath.'

'Panic?' suggested Harker, gently.

'That's why I say it's possible . . . just.'

Harker nodded genuine appreciation. This man *was* honest. With most people, the suggestion would have brought at least mild indignation. Outrage even. To hint that a man's father might have lied about the manner in which his mother met her death was a tricky business, but this tall, slightly gangling man was wise enough to meet the possible truth head-on, and give a very honest answer.

They sipped coffee for a moment, then Harker moved the conversation a notch farther along the lines he wished it to take.

'Tell me about your father,' he said quietly.

'I'm sorry?' Duxbury looked puzzled.

'The sort of man he is.'

'He's a good father. Always has been. He built this firm up from nothing. That's a monument to what sort of man he is.'

'Industrious?'

'That goes without saying.'

'Friendly?'

'Too friendly sometimes. Friendly to the point of weakness.'

Harker smiled non-understanding.

'Look, sergeant.' Duxbury replaced his cup on the table. 'This is a typical family business. Father always wanted it that way. Still wants it that way. But he goes to extremes. He tends to treat every employee as *part* of his family.' Duxbury moved his shoulders in gentle resignation. 'It has its advantages, of course. We've never had any disputes. Very rarely do we get slipshod work. Those we employ, if they know their job, stay. Years. We've men who started here from school . . . they'll probably retire, without working for any other firm.' He leaned forward and re-filled his cup from the tall coffee-pot, as he continued, 'That's on the credit side, but there's another side.' He spooned sugar into the coffee, then added a tiny portion of cream. He straightened as he stirred. 'It's human nature, I suppose, but some of them think they *can't* be sacked. They talk to him as an equal – they talk to *me* as an equal – and that's okay. It's hard to put into words. I don't want lickspittle . . . just the tacit understanding that it's *our* firm. We're solid, but these days . . .' He sipped the coffee. 'Good firms are going to the wall. Suddenly. Without warning. If *we* go bust, *we* suffer. The skilled operatives – a personal opinion, of course – they won't stay unemployed for too long. *We'll* be left holding the baby.'

'They don't appreciate that?' Harker teased Duxbury into continuing the conversation.

'Some do, but most of them don't. I can give you two instances. A man called Evans. He'd been here about two years. November – November the third – I was stock-taking and it didn't come out right. Not by a country mile. I asked around. Evans had been robbing us blind . . .'

He told the story of Evans and the confrontation with John Duxbury. He told it in a tight, hard voice, as if he still held a grudge against his father for not calling in the police.

The story was a long way from a certain cliff edge, but it was what Harker had been praying for. Off at a tangent. A tangent which hinted at the personality of John Duxbury. A weak man, perhaps? A man too good to be true? A man who yearned for popularity at any price? Harker was a copper, with a copper's natural suspicion. Angels were at a premium on this earth. They didn't come by the carton. Clip the wings. Dent the halo. You sometimes got the shock of your life.

'. . . He should have sent for you people,' ended Duxbury. 'It was theft, pure and simple.'

'What happened to Evans?' asked Harker.

'Last I heard – last week, I think – he left the district. He got a job down south. Plymouth way somewhere. They're welcome to him.'

'And the other thing?' coaxed Harker.

'What?'

'You said you could give two examples.'

172

'Oh, that?' Duxbury smiled, then tasted his coffee. 'Not quite the same thing, of course. What I was getting at – the instance I had in mind – that the men often think the work comes to *us*. They do the work. Good work. But it has to be almost touted for. The major London publishing houses. Especially those specialising in the coffee-table editions. They pay well, but naturally they choose carefully. The competition to print is very keen. It was – er,' he leaned across and slid a diary from the surface of the desk, consulted it and continued, 'yes. Mid-November. November the sixteenth. A Tuesday. Father had to travel down to Saffron Walden to meet one of the directors of a London publishing house.' He closed the diary and tossed it back onto the desk. 'I call that touting, but necessary. Something the men on the shop floor don't see. But without it, they'd be out of a job.'

'Did he get the contract?' asked Harker with a smile.

'I think we have. A couple more weeks and we should know.'

'Therefore, whatever other weakness he has, he's a good businessman.'

'He has patience. Far more patience than I have.'

'You *wouldn't* have gone all that way?'

'Oh, yes,' said Duxbury hurriedly. 'A good hotel. The Saffron. I was prepared to go with him, but he thought it better to go alone.'

'Why?'

'I – er – I tend to be blunt. Too blunt sometimes.'

'So he recognises *your* weaknesses?'

'I suppose so.' Duxbury chuckled quietly. 'I hadn't thought about it that way. He can be a wily bird sometimes.'

Harker drained his cup and replaced it on the table before he spoke again.

'We seem to have got off track,' he said and the apologetic tone sounded genuine.

'I'm sorry. My fault as much as yours.'

'Not at all.' Harker consulted his open notebook, then said, 'Your mother.'

'Yes?'

'I have to ask these questions. As I've explained. Coroners . . .'

'That's quite all right.'

'Depression?' said Harker gently.

'I'm sorry?'

'Women of a certain age . . . they tend to have bouts of depression.'

'Not mother.'

'You'd know? I mean, you *would* know?'

'Most certainly. I knew my mother very well indeed.'

'So, we can rule out – er – suicide?'

'Definitely.'

'Not – er – ' The mock-embarrassment was beautifully enacted. He even rubbed his lips with a forefinger. 'Not for other reasons either?'

'Sergeant, please ask the questions you're required to ask,' said Duxbury.

'Y'see,' said Harker, awkwardly, 'marriages don't always last. One or the other . . .'

'She wasn't having an affair,' said Duxbury bluntly.

'Ah!'

'Nor was my father.'

'It – er – it does happen,' muttered Harker. 'Sometimes with tragic consequences.'

'Not with *my* parents.'

'Thanks.' Harker scribbled words in his notebook. Without looking up he asked, 'What was she like?'

'Mother?'

'Did you know her as well as you know your father?' He looked up as he asked the question.

'Naturally.'

'You worked with him, of course. Here. Every day.'

'I knew her just as well.'

'What was she like?'

'She's dead,' said Duxbury flatly.

'Quite. That makes an objective assessment difficult.'

'Not really.' Duxbury paused, then went on, 'She was very strong-willed.'

'Strong-willed?'

'Difficult . . . at times.'

Harker frowned non-understanding.

'You see.' Duxbury took a deep breath. 'People thought father was hen-pecked. He wasn't. Not really. He had the right temperament. He never lost his patience. Even when she was at her worst, he merely smiled and allowed the moment to pass without comment.'

'She was as bad as that sometimes?'

'She was . . .' Duxbury nodded. 'Yes, she was pretty awful sometimes.'

'And your father never lost his temper?'

'Never.'

'I never married,' observed Harker, conversationally. 'But I remember my own parents. Average, I suppose. Better than most, maybe. But they had rows occasionally. Tiredness. Moodiness. Nothing titanic. No blows. No throwing things. But – just now and again – they had some almighty rows.'

'Who doesn't?' Duxbury chuckled. 'Ben and I – Ben's my wife – at it like cat and dog for a few minutes . . . then we laugh. It's part of being in love.'

'Your parents didn't,' said Harker gently. Pointedly.

The chuckle turned to a lop-sided grin, and Duxbury said, 'Meaning they *weren't* in love?'

'A thought,' said Harker off-handedly.

'He's fifty years old. Mother wasn't much younger.'

'The gilt's off the gingerbread?'

'Some of it must be.' Then Duxbury added, 'Mustn't it?'

'There's the "growing old gracefully" gag.'

'Not with mother, I'm afraid.'

'No?'

'I think, secretly, she hated growing older. Much as she hated illness. She had this thing about "uncleanliness" . . . as she called it.'

'Uhu.' Harker waited.

'Not just untidiness. Y'know, the untidiness of a real home. A home that's lived in. She went further than that. Much further. It was almost a phobia. Cleanliness!' He smiled a little sadly. 'Operating theatres were filthy by comparison.'

'What about holidays?' asked Harker innocently. 'Hotels?'

'They never had a holiday. For ten years – more – they never slept other than in their own beds. I – er – I suspect she got worse as she grew older. This "cleanliness" thing. This last one. This last weekend thing . . .' He paused to clear his throat and frown. 'It was my idea. If I hadn't insisted . . . Daft I know. But it brings on a sense of guilt.'

'It's not your fault they walked along the edge of that cliff.'

'Nevertheless . . .'

There was a short silence, as if in token respect for the dead Maude Duxbury.

'Your father didn't mind?' said Harker.

'What?'

'About never having a holiday?'

'He had this firm. It was his life. All he ever wanted.'

'Still . . .' Harker left the sentence incompleted.

'He's a strange man.' Duxbury seemed to be voicing his thoughts, rather than answering the implied question. 'Unique. He never complained. Never asked much out of life. I'd say . . . tranquil. That's the nearest I can get to it. Tranquil. But more than that. He never showed disappointment. Never showed enthusiasm. Anger. *Anything*.'

'Happiness?' suggested Harker.

'I suppose he was happy,' mused Duxbury. 'He was never *un*happy. Never miserable.'

'Didn't show it?'

'I – er – I suppose that's what it boils down to. Everybody feels things. Feels emotion one way or another. Father too, I suppose. He *must*. He just has this great capacity for not showing it.'

Past tense. Present tense. Harker didn't miss the subtlety. An unconscious subtlety. Sometimes Duxbury's words suggested that his father, too, was dead. Past tense. Then he seemed to remember, and dropped back into the present tense; remembering that his father was still alive.

The conversational relationship between the two men had changed. There was a closeness. An intimacy. A rapport, well beyond that of policeman and stranger. In truth, Harker didn't *look* like a policeman. The tweed suit, the walking-stick, even the limp. The way he spoke. Gently, as if in confidence. No hint of bombast. Instead, what appeared to be genuine interest. To say they were already friends – even good friends – would not be an exaggeration. That on the surface . . . and probably below the surface. It was the way Harker had planned it, but Duxbury had met him half-way. As if the younger man needed somebody with whom he could talk. Somebody to whom he could open up his heart. Somebody whom he could trust.

Harker . . . the epitome of the 'favourite uncle' figure.

And why not?

Duxbury was suffering the backlash of an emotional upheaval. He needed a prop. Something – somebody – to help take the strain.

He lowered his eyes, stared at the carpet for a moment, then muttered, 'I don't think they loved each other.'

'They were past the first flush of youth,' observed Harker gently. 'People at that age don't often exhibit . . .'

'No!' Duxbury interrupted, raised his head and looked at Harker. There was sadness at the back of his eyes. He said, 'I don't mean age. I remember as a kid. Kids notice these things. They're not supposed to, but they do. Maybe they don't even know what it is they notice. Just *something*. There wasn't much laughter. No "in" jokes, family jokes . . . like Ben and I have. Just politeness. No laughter. No love.'

'They – er – they didn't quarrel.'

'No. You don't quarrel with an armchair. With a standard lamp. It's there. It's useful. Decorative. But you don't hate it, you don't love it. It's just part of the room. Part of the house.'

Harker said, 'You're sure you're not being wise after the event?'

'Oh, *I* loved them,' continued Duxbury in a sad, faraway tone. 'I loved them both. I just couldn't understand why they didn't love each other.'

'They loved you?'

'Of course.' Duxbury seemed amazed that the question should be asked. 'Especially father. As I've already said, he wasn't demonstrative. Still isn't. Nothing you could put your finger on, but even as a kid I knew. It was there. Always. We were *comfortable* in each other's company. More like pals than father and son. Still are.'

'But your mother not quite as much . . . you think,' probed Harker.

'There was always a certain – how can I put it? – a certain . . .

177

edginess.' His voice lowered. He was criticising his mother, and his mother had just died a violent death. Nevertheless, he continued, 'I can talk to you, much easier than I could talk to her. She always "knew best" . . . you know what I mean. I – er – I don't think she meant it to be so. It was just her way. But I was never as near to her as I was to father.'

'And now she's dead?' said Harker gently.

'I . . .' He swallowed. 'I wish I'd tried harder. I wish I'd tried to understand a little more.'

'Understand what?'

'That . . .' For a moment he was at a loss for words. He chewed his lower lip, then murmured, 'That she was a very unhappy woman. Basically. I think that's what it boiled down to.'

'Unhappy?'

'I've already said. They didn't *love* each other. It was all a pretence. Years. Year after year. This everlasting pretence of being happily married. She *had* to be unhappy.'

'Shyness, perhaps?' teased Harker. 'You took it to be unhappiness, when in fact it was shyness.'

'She wasn't shy,' said Duxbury firmly. 'Just occasionally we had parties – went to parties – she enjoyed herself.' He hesitated, then added, 'She particularly enjoyed the company of men. Not flirting. Not *that*. Just a – a sort of rebellion against father. Something of that sort.'

'And your father? At parties, I mean.'

'As always. He never changed. Quiet. Uncommunicative.'

'But your mother wasn't a flirt?'

'Definitely not.' There was no hint of doubt in the reply. 'I'm not a child anymore. I've seen her. Watched her. Friendly arguments . . . that's what she enjoyed. Conversation. But not the usual "women's talk". Father couldn't give her it. Or *wouldn't*. But that's all it was. She became another woman. Vital. Alive. Laughing, even. But the minute we got back to the car – or when the last guest left – it was like turning off a switch.' Then, in a burst of anger and anguish, 'Why in hell's name did they marry each other in the first place?'

'People make mistakes,' comforted Harker.

'I know. But *what* a mistake.' A pause – a long pause – then a muttered, 'The wonder is one of them didn't kill the other.'

'So much hatred?' Harker knew he was stepping on egg-shells.

'No *love*. Not even respect. Nothing!'

'Would it have surprised you?' said Harker carefully.

'What?'

'If one had killed the other.' Then hurriedly, 'Not shock. Of course it would have shocked you. But would it have *surprised* you?'

A frown creased Duxbury's brow as he gave the question sombre consideration. Harker watched, and wondered how far he dare go.

'I don't think it would.' Duxbury spoke slowly, as if the admission was having to be forced from his lips. 'As you say . . . shock. But not surprise. Not *real* surprise.' A long, deep sigh, then, 'I don't have to tell you. People have killed for a lot less.'

'For a lot less,' agreed Harker . . . and left it at that.

The talk continued for perhaps half an hour longer. Harker was wise enough to step back from the brink. Already he'd learned more than he'd ever hoped to learn. He liked this man, Harry Duxbury. He liked him, and was saddened at the hurt likely to be inflicted on him before the end of the enquiry. Because the enquiry was going to continue. It *had* to continue. Too many loose ends had been knotted and put into place. John and Maude Duxbury were now more than names. They were personalities . . . each, it seemed, capable of murder.

They shook hands as Harker left and Duxbury said, 'Anything else – anything else the coroner wants to know – don't hesitate.'

'Thanks.' Then, almost as an afterthought. 'It's more than possible.'

PART TWELVE

The Tenacity of Harry Harker

The glimmer was there. The possibility. The highly-unlikely, thousand-to-one chance, but it was *there*.

That, plus the gut feeling, and the gut feeling was important. Very important. Ask any good thief-taker, and he'll tell you he *knows*. But, don't ask him how he knows, because that he *doesn't* know. How does the man in the circus cage know that a previously well-behaved big cat is about to turn nasty? How does a man who's spent his life at sea know, without gadgetry, that foul weather is beyond the horizon? How does the farmer know, by running the soil between his fingers, whether the crop will be better or worse than it was last year? Experience? Ah yes, but experience plus. Experience honed to a razor-sharp cutting edge, therefore more than experience. An extra sense. An extra certainty. That which separates the merely good from the great.

Harker knew. Harker would have bet his life on it.

Having left Harry Duxbury, he sat in the car and pondered upon his next move.

Rimstone took some finding, but having found the village which gave its name to the beat, the police house was there, with its illuminated sign, for all to see. Pinter was at home and, having introduced himself, Harker was invited into the tiny office, the wall gas-fire was lighted and the two talked and planned.

Pinter told all he'd learned since being contacted by Tallboy. Harker listened, nodded satisfied understanding now and again, but didn't interrupt.

'And that's about it,' ended Pinter. 'The gaffer told me to start nosing around. That you might be in touch. That's as far as he

183

went.'

'Murder,' said Harker flatly. And there was no 'might be' qualification attached to the word.

Pinter looked interested, but not surprised.

'You don't need smelling salts.' Harker's observation was drily sardonic.

Pinter said, 'A chief superintendent rings a village bobby. Tells him as little as possible, but wants griff for a detective sergeant from another force. That doesn't equate with a dog without a licence.'

'Clever lad,' smiled Harker.

'It also means you're either not sure or can't prove.'

'I'm sure.'

'His wife fell over a cliff,' mused Pinter. 'At a guess she *didn't* fall over a cliff.'

'Observations,' invited Harker.

'Who *doesn't* feel like murder?' said Pinter sombrely. 'My wife died. I could have murdered God Himself. Everybody . . . at some time or another. With most people it goes away. With some people it happens before it has a chance to go away.'

'Oh, very erudite.'

'You asked.'

'Uhu . . . and Duxbury?'

'He's "people". No better than me. No worse.'

'What about his late missus?'

'I wasn't married to her.'

'You're a chary bugger.'

'I don't speculate. I've asked around, as ordered. Now you know as much as I do.'

'This diary thing?' asked Harker. 'Do you believe the cleaning woman?'

'She exaggerates,' said Pinter. 'But I don't think she deliberately lies.'

'The word "diary". It can mean anything.'

'A lot more comprehensive than a list of appointments. That's the impression I got.'

'Ah, but she exaggerates.'

Pinter nodded.

Harker said, 'It might be worth looking at.'

'It might also be a waste of time. Nobody records committing murder.'

'True.' Harker rubbed his jaw for a moment, then made up his mind. 'There's a man called Evans. Worked at Duxbury's place until early November. He was sacked for nicking things. He's moved out of the district. Down south somewhere. I'd like his present address . . . without Duxbury or his son knowing. Think you can do it?'

'I'll do it,' promised Pinter.

'Good.' Harker hoisted himself upright with the aid of his walking stick. 'Tomorrow. Say five o'clock, at Div. Headquarters.'

'I'll be there.'

Tallboy was still in his office, putting the finishing touches to a long day's paperwork. A practical copper, he loathed the massive pile of bumpf which, every morning, was dumped in his In-tray, but he was divisional officer and, present-day policing being what it is, every can from Beechwood Brook had to carry his personal signature of approval.

He waved Harker into a chair, flexed his slightly cramped fingers and leaned back from the desk.

'Any luck?' he asked.

'It could be fool's gold,' said Harker carefully.

'What's that mean?'

'It means,' said Harker, 'you have a murderer in your division. It also means he has a better than evens chance of getting away with it.'

'I'd like the details,' said Tallboy.

Harker told him. Everything. The smattering of facts, plus the mountain of near-certainties beyond reach of any proof. Tallboy punctuated the telling with an occasional pointed question, and Harker's answers were equally pointed.

'Still, it's nice to know,' said Tallboy, resignedly. 'If *we* know, and he doesn't *know* we know, he might take a second bite of the apple at some time in the future.'

'Not good enough, sir.'

'As I see things, it *has* to be good enough.'

185

Quietly, calmly, Harker said, 'I'm going to interview him.'

'Crack him?' There was a hint of sarcasm in the question.

'Smash him,' said Harker, flatly. 'In front of his son.'

'What good will that do?'

'The way I see things.' Harker's eyes were hard and uncompromising. 'Every man has a reputation. Duxbury has. A nice guy. A very honest guy. An upright citizen. The hell he is! He's a killer. Okay, we can't prove it in court . . . not yet. But *if* we can't prove it in court, I'll destroy that reputation as far as the one person whose opinion he respects is concerned.'

'Is that our job?' asked Tallboy gently.

'With or without your blessing, chief superintendent.'

'I asked . . . is that our job?'

'It's justice,' growled Harker. 'Sod the law books. Sod the judge and the jury. As *I* see it, we're here to tame the wrong-doers. I won't step beyond the law – I value my pension too much for that – but I'll make damn sure the law gives me elbow-room enough to make him wish he *had* made a mistake. Make him wish the only thing he *has* to worry about is a spell inside.'

'And if he denies everything?'

'I'll call him a liar. I'll find fifty thousand different ways of calling him a liar.'

'And if he *still* denies it?'

'I'll get Foster down here. I'll confront them with each other. I'll make damn sure one of them breaks.'

'All worked out,' sighed Tallboy. 'The copper with an obsession . . . there's *always* a way.'

'Sir.' Harker's tone softened slightly. 'One murderer versus one detective sergeant. Outside badly-written whodunnits, it very rarely happens. This time, that's *just* what it boils down to. And the murderer's winning. He's pushed me into a cul-de-sac. No way out except to turn round and go home, and that I *won't* do. My only option. To force a way through the dead-end of that cul-de-sac, and drag the bastard with me. I either can or I can't, but, by God, I'm going to try!'

Tallboy nodded slowly. A reluctant acknowledgement.

'What next?' he asked.

'I'm meeting Pinter here tomorrow. Five o'clock.'

'Then?'

'I meet John Duxbury.'

'With Pinter?'

'With Pinter, and with his son, Harry Duxbury.'

'*And* with me,' said Tallboy grimly.

Harker nodded.

'What good will it do?' asked Tallboy.

'I don't know.' Harker's twisted grin was rueful. 'Just that between now and then I'm going to check everything I know about him. Every damn thing. He's not perfect. There has to be a flaw.'

'A way through the cul-de-sac?' smiled Tallboy.

'If there is, I'll find it.'

This time, Tallboy nodded.

'You can do me a favour,' said Harker. 'A search warrant might come in handy.'

'On what grounds?'

'Suspected murder.'

'Good God, man, you can't expect . . .'

'That's what it is,' insisted Harker. 'I want to get *into* the house. I want the authority. No fannying around on the doorstep. No bluff. I want the authority to *tell* him . . . not *ask* him. And when I'm inside, I want the authority to look for things. Specifically that diary.'

'You think the diary's important?'

'I'll tell you when I've read it.'

'You're cutting things very fine, sergeant.'

'Yes, sir,' agreed Harker.

'We have . . .' Tallboy hesitated, then said, 'We have a very understanding magistrate.'

Harker waited.

Tallboy said, 'You'll have your search warrant. Just don't make me look *too* big a fool.'

The previous day had not been a very easy day for Harker. He'd tended to wallow in self-pity a little. Almost gone home with his tail between his legs.

But that had been yesterday, when the object of the whole exercise, and the *main* object of the exercise, had seemed to have been the saving of Briggs's stupid neck. More importantly, that had been before Harker's meeting with Harry Duxbury and before the exchange of views with Police Constable Pinter.

Harry Duxbury and P.C. Pinter had made all the difference. They'd flipped the coin, and now to hell with Briggs – things had become very personal.

Harker topped up the Fiesta's tank, then drove fast to the hotel. Raymond and Martha Foster were in their bedroom, but hadn't yet retired. They were reading and, as Harker entered, they both looked up with the same worried expression.

Foster began, 'I – I thought . . .'

His wife spoke at the same time. 'Sergeant, can't you please . . .'

'Shut up, the pair of you.' Harker limped to a bed and sat down. He pointed a stiffened finger at Foster. 'Last time of asking. You're *sure?*'

'Of course I'm sure,' groaned Foster. 'But I don't want . . .'

'That's not important,' snapped Harker.

'It's *very* important.' The woman's tone matched Harker's. 'If you think . . .'

'Get in my way. Either of you.' Harker switched his glare from one to the other. 'Get in the way, and I'll walk over you. Murder may have a place in your precious scheme of life. It hasn't a place in mine. I'm here to verify. To make *bloody* sure.'

'I don't lie,' breathed Foster.

'Or make mistakes?'

'Not this time. He pushed her over. I swear . . . he pushed her over the edge.'

'You'll take an oath on that?'

'If – if I have to. But . . .'

'In a witness box?'

'Oh, my God!'

'*In a witness box?*' snarled Harker.

'If – if I have to.'

'You won't have to.' There was spitting contempt in his voice, as he said, 'I wouldn't put you – either of you – in a witness box to give evidence that a straight line has two ends.'

'That's a disgusting thing to . . .'

'Shut up, lady. Just be glad *somebody* has the job of keeping the

188

predators under control while you people enjoy your nut cutlets.'

It was a come on of course. As he'd said, a 'verification'. Scare the living daylights out of the weak-kneed bastard. Make him think his world was tumbling around his ears. If he *still* stuck to his original story, that last hint of doubt had been taken care of.

Harker pushed the Fiesta south at a steady sixty, and figured that being a copper was, on the whole, a dirty business. Nice people. Stupid, but innocent. Ridiculously honest. But the job required you to put on a 'demon king' routine in order to double-check that honesty.

He made for Leeds and the motorways. The 'Motorway City' with a maze of under-passes and fly-overs. Strip-lighted tunnels which swooped up into the open air, higher than housetops, then plunged down into the neon-lit earth again. Dozens of road signs. Hundreds! Miss one and you were way and gone to hell off track. Follow the blue signs. The blue signs kept you on the motorway network, and only on motorways could you be sure of all-night filling stations.

no wonder we got lost!

Once on the M1 he eased the speed a little. It was December, with a few degrees of frost in the air. He drove into and out of sporadic downpours of sleet and rain. The gritters hadn't yet been out, and black ice was at least a possibility. Black ice. The bloody stuff that gave the appearance of a simple, wet road surface but it was as impossible to negotiate as any skid-pan. He had a destination, but he wanted to *reach* that destination.

South of Junction 15, he pulled into the service area, parked the car and hobbled into the all-night café. Hot soup and bread-buns at a ridiculous price. A group of long-distance boys playing cards at one of the tables; easing the strain of the throb of engines, prior to continuing their roar through the night. Teenagers, pale-faced and sullen, waiting over cups of already-cold tea for somebody to offer them a lift. That strange, gritty taste in the mouth, peculiar to the small hours.

Harker sat and eased the stiffness from his bones and (again) his mood fluctuated. Oh, sure, it had developed into a straight fight between himself and John Duxbury, but was it worth it? Two middle-aged men who hadn't even yet met. The chances were Duxbury hadn't even *heard* of Detective Sergeant Harker. So who was the damn fool? Duxbury, comfortable in his own bed? Or him (Harker) with a hell of a drive behind him, and another hell of a drive yet to come, and for what? A night without sleep, a long drive ahead, one more brick wall at the end of the cul-de-sac, then a long drive back. Who the hell *was* the mug?

Murder? So what? Murders are committed every day. Week in, week out, year in, year out. Murder. Some aren't even recognised as murder. Dozens of them remain undetected . . . or undetectable. What the hell was so different about Maude Duxbury's murder? A woman, pushed over a cliff. Big deal! People fell from cliffs all the time. People died from falls from cliffs all the time. That – or so it seemed – was what cliffs were for. To fall from. To be pushed from.

So, why the hell was he (Harry Harker) driving himself to the point of exhaustion?

Personal, eh?

Sure, that was it. Man against man, instead of the usual man against machine. Like a heavyweight championship of the world. Murder. The top cherry. Forget all the gewgaws the Police Service had at its disposal. This time they didn't count. This time it was Harker versus Duxbury. Therefore, personal. The hell he was going to be licked by some hick-town printer. The *hell* he was!

He consulted the road map he'd brought from the car with him then, having decided the route, he re-folded the map, reached for his walking stick and hobbled back to the car.

He left the motorway and drove east. Along the A422, then right and south of Bedford. The A603 brought him to the A1, and there he turned south. Then left, along unclassified roads. Slower driving, past Edworth, and Hinxworth and Ashwell. Following the signposts and not the road numbers. Then east, along the A505 and, south of Royston, right and along the B1039. He'd topped up the fuel tank at the service area, and it had been a wise thing to do. Strange, winding roads. Strange, unknown villages, still sleeping. Barley and Great Chisill. Wendens Ambo then under the M11 and past Audley End. Third gear work much of the time, with his eyes aching a little and his head throbbing a little. It would be better on the return journey. Filling stations would be open, and he could stick to A-class roads and easier driving.

It was past dawn when he arrived at his destination. A market town whose whole economy had once been built on a Greek wild flower which had been introduced to the district by Thomas Smith, secretary of state to King Edward VI. An old town, whose narrow high street was lined with picturesque buildings. Not a town planned for motor cars, and he zig-zagged around side roads until he found a parking place. Then he switched off the engine, tilted back the driving seat and cat-napped, pending the appearance of enough pedestrians to ensure that most of the inhabitants were awake.

He left the car, limped stiffly back to the high street and found the main hotel. On production of his warrant card, his questions were answered. He was given facilities to wash and freshen himself up, then served with a fine breakfast.

Then it was back to Beechwood Brook . . . having found nothing he hadn't known before his arrival.

A long, hot soak, a shave, a clean shirt, clean socks and clean underclothes and he was as fit as any man of his age could hope to be having missed a night's sleep and driven all of four hundred miles. He was at Beechwood Brook D.H.Q. at five o'clock, on the button, and Police Constable Pinter was waiting for him.

'That's as far as I can get.'

Pinter sounded disappointed as he handed him a picture postcard. It was a view of Plymouth Hoe, and carried a Plymouth postmark.

Pinter continued, 'Evans sent it to his landlady where he was lodging. No address, and she doesn't know the address.'

'So why keep in touch?' Harker turned the postcard as he spoke.

'He owes her money. She doesn't think he'll ever pay, but the postcard is a sweetener to keep her quiet a bit longer. That's what *she* thinks.'

'And what do *you* think?'

'I think he's bedded her a few times, and this is his way of saying "Take off, sweetheart".'

'So why send it?'

'*And* owes her money.'

'He's a mug,' muttered Harker.

'And without taste.'

'That's an unkind remark to make, constable.'

'Yes, sergeant.' Pinter allowed a smile to touch his lips, then added, 'The gaffer's waiting for us in his office.'

They strolled along the corridors, knocked on the door and entered Tallboy's office. Tallboy was waiting for them, nodded a silent greeting, then picked a folded, foolscap-size document from the desk and handed it to Harker.

'Your search warrant,' he said shortly.

Harker took the warrant and tucked it, together with the postcard, into the inside pocket of his jacket.

'Sit down . . . both of you.' There was a terseness in Tallboy's tone which went with the full chief superintendent's regalia he was wearing. He waited until they were seated, then continued, 'Sergeant. A few things to be made clear before we go out to Rimstone.'

Harker waited.

Tallboy continued, 'I pull the plug if I think you're going too far. Understood?'

'No, sir,' said Harker quietly. '*Not* understood.'

'You say he's a murderer.'

'I *know* he's a murderer.'

'*I* say we haven't enough evidence to hang a cat.'

'We don't disagree,' growled Harker.

'Therefore, no harassment.'

'Murder . . . but not harassment?' There was open mockery in Harker's question.

'If I say "Enough", that's it,' snapped Tallboy.

'Chief Superintendent Tallboy.' Harker's voice was rock-steady. His gaze met Tallboy's unwaveringly. 'A murder has been committed in *my* police district. That – I don't have to remind you – gives me full authority to question who I like, when I like, in *any* police district. You hold a rank, but that rank is limited to *your* police district. To the officers under *your* authority. Not to me. To me, it's just a courtesy title. I'll give it the courtesy it's due. But I'm damned if I'll take orders – be told what to do or how to do it – from a man who hasn't the authority to *give* those orders. Police Constable Pinter, here, you can say "enough" to him. Not me. As far as *I'm* concerned, you're just an onlooker. I'll stay within the law, but if harassment is required, I'll harass. By God, I'll harass! And you won't stop me, because you *can't* stop me.'

'You're a brave man, sergeant,' said Tallboy in a low voice.

'Maybe.'

'Or a very foolish man.'

'Maybe that, too.'

'I *have* been known to misplace the book of rules.'

'Yes, sir,' said Harker politely. 'We're all forgetful at times.'

Pinter's eyes moved between the faces of the two men. He knew he'd just witnessed a minor battle of giants. Tallboy was no patsy. His past record – his reputation – was enough to make most sergeants quake a little. But this stranger – this Harker – had issued an outright challenge. Calmly, and without fuss, he'd put Tallboy firmly in his legal niche . . . and all three knew it.

In the silence following the exchange, Tallboy lighted a cigarette. The lighter flame was steady. There wasn't a waver from the thread of smoke which rose from the burning tobacco.

Almost conversationally, he said, 'Seven o'clock, sergeant. At Duxbury's place. I've arranged for his son Harry to be there. We'll meet up. I'll see you both there.'

'Yes, sir.' Harker hoiked himself from the chair. 'I'll take Constable Pinter in my car.'

PART THIRTEEN

The Ordeal of John Duxbury

Pinter said, 'He's a good gaffer, sergeant.'

'Is he?' Harker leaned forward slightly, as far as the seat belt would allow, and peered past the switching blades of the wipers and into the drizzle-drenched rays of the headlamps. 'Above a certain rank, they're all good. Useless, but good.'

'He'll back you in a tight corner.' Pinter was eager to ensure that Harker hadn't the wrong impression of Tallboy. Harker grunted. Pinter continued, 'I know. He has with me, more than once.'

Harker concentrated on driving. They were on unlit country lanes, and the drizzle was as thick as a mist.

'He took over from Blayde.'

'Who the hell's Blayde?'

'Chief Superintendent Blayde.'

'Never heard of him.'

Harker's professed ignorance was a lie. Blayde had been something of a legend and even Harker, whose natural impulse veered towards the debunking of legends, had heard and marvelled at stories of Chief Superintendent Robert Blayde. But he was a stranger in a strange land. Well away from his own midden. Who was his friend? Who was his foe? More importantly, who was his foe masquerading as his friend? The safest bet was to trust nobody.

They drove in silence until they reached the house. A Rover was parked on the grass verge, opposite the drive. In the drive stood a Volvo, and Harker recognised it as one of a handful of cars which had been parked in the yard of the printing works. Harker parked the Fiesta behind the Rover.

Tallboy climbed from the Rover and they met as a group just off the wet grass.

'Everything rehearsed, sergeant?' asked Tallboy. Harker didn't answer, and Tallboy continued, 'The son's already here. He was here when I arrived.'

They crossed the lane, walked up the drive and Tallboy pressed the bell-push.

Harry Duxbury opened the door, greeted Tallboy as a friend, then stood aside to allow them to pass.

Harker entered last, and Duxbury smiled and murmured, 'So soon, sergeant.'

'Some things are necessary.' Harker's face was expressionless, but the tone carried the suggestion of an apology. 'Necessary, but sometimes not nice.'

The lounge was both huge and luxurious. It housed a sofa large enough to seat four people, four matching armchairs, an assortment of matching upright chairs and ottomans and half a dozen low tables of differing sizes. It required the furniture to prevent itself looking bare. It needed the ceiling-to-floor drapes at the windows. The scattering of Persian-style rugs. The mock-Adam fireplace, with its heavy square fire-basket in which blazed split logs and coal cobbles. The back-up heat of long, low double-radiators. The twin, four-bulb ceiling lights, plus the half-dozen wall-lights. Without all these things, plus lesser appurtenances, the room would have looked vulgar and larger than it was required to look. With them, the balance was just right.

Harker sat in an armchair to the right of the fireplace. John Duxbury faced him, at a slight angle, in the armchair on the left of the fireplace. Tallboy and Harry Duxbury shared the sofa, each sitting at one end. Pinter was in a third armchair, slightly behind the sofa and between the sofa and John Duxbury's chair.

A little awkwardly, Duxbury said, 'Chris rang. Said you'd like to see me.'

'Chris?' Harker pretended puzzlement.

'Chris Tallboy.' He was plump, rather than stout. Clean-shaven. Almost shiny. He was almost completely bald, and this added to the shiny effect. His voice was pleasant. Friendly. As if he'd *taught* himself to be friendly, whatever the occasion. 'Chief Superintendent Tallboy. We know each ·other. Respect each other.'

'I'm not on first-name terms with chief superintendents,' said
Harker. Then, 'Did "Chris" explain the reason for my wanting to
see you?'

'I did.' Harry Duxbury answered the question. 'I told him it was
about mother's accident. There doesn't seem to be any other
reason.'

'*Is* that why you're here?' asked Duxbury.

'The death of your wife,' agreed Harker evasively.

'Three of you?' Duxbury moved his head, and gave a half-smile
to each in turn. 'A chief superintendent. The local constable. And
you, a detective sergeant. It suggests grave doubt.' He held
Harker's eyes for a moment, then added, 'About something.'

'About certain aspects,' said Tallboy quietly.

'You're here in uniform, Chris. I take it that means an "official"
visit?'

'I'm afraid so.'

'I thought I'd cleared up all the points yesterday.' Harry
Duxbury gave Harker a sad and disappointed look. 'In order *not* to
upset dad more than was necessary.'

'Not everything,' said Harker. 'You couldn't. You weren't there
when it happened.'

'When she fell over the cliff?' said Duxbury.

'When she died.'

'That's what I mean. When she . . .'

'Just you and her,' interrupted Harker gently. 'You can tell me
things nobody else knows.'

'Of course.' Duxbury nodded benignly. 'And of course, will.'

'Was she dead?' Harker was anxious to get the mock-
convivialities out of the way. 'When she landed, was she dead?'

'I – I don't really know.' The shock of the question drove colour
from Duxbury's face.

'You looked down at her?'

'Yes. Of course I . . .'

'Did she move?'

'No.'

'Just lay there?'

'Y-yes.'

199

'No noise? No moaning?'

'No.'

'Nothing?'

'No . . . nothing.'

'Look, I really think . . .' Harry Duxbury's tone was both angry and concerned. 'I suppose you have to do these things, but . . .'

'It's necessary,' said Tallboy. 'There's no polite or easy way of asking these questions.'

Harry Duxbury sighed deeply, but closed his mouth. Harker ignored the interruption and continued.

'Remember the Fosters?'

'The – er – the . . .'

'The Fosters? They were staying at the same hotel.'

'Oh, yes.' Duxbury gave a single nod. 'A young couple. He – er – he objected to me smoking.'

'The two stories don't tally,' said Harker flatly.

'The two . . .'

'Their version and your version.'

'I – I don't see how . . .'

'Bird-watching enthusiasts.'

'The Fosters? Yes, I remember. He said something about it.'

'They saw it happen.' It was a little like prodding a timid animal with a stick. 'They were out . . . bird-watching. In a makeshift hide. They had binoculars. They saw what happened.'

'Oh!'

'You and your wife. They had a clear view. They saw *exactly* what happened.'

Harry Duxbury exploded, 'In that case, why the devil didn't they *do* something?'

'What for example?' Harker turned a tired gaze upon the younger man.

'They could have – they could have . . .' He stopped and spread his opened hands. Like an angler, gradually exaggerating the size of a catch. 'They could have done *something*.'

'Climbed down? To check that she wasn't still alive?'

'Yes.' He grasped the suggestion eagerly. 'They could have done that.'

'Your father didn't.'

'He's – he's not a young man. He isn't energetic, like . . .'

'We're talking about *his* wife.'

'All right! All right! They could have . . . shouted. Let him know they were there.'

'Your father didn't do that either.'

'What?'

'Shout.'

'If he was alone – thought he was alone – what good would that have . . .'

'He didn't shout down to your mother. To check that she might still be alive, and able to answer.'

'It's all right, Harry.' Duxbury ran the palm of a hand across his baldness. 'They couldn't have done anything.' Then to Harker, 'Why weren't they called at the inquest?'

'They would have been, had we known.'

'Known?' Duxbury looked puzzled.

'You've met them.' Harker's lips curled. 'They tend towards the shrinking violet way of life.'

'You found them then . . . after the inquest.'

'They found *us*.'

'Oh!'

'They told their story. You'd told your story. The two didn't match.'

Duxbury said, 'Oh!' again. He moved his shoulders resignedly. 'That's *really* why you're here. To check out the inconsistencies.'

'In a nutshell,' agreed Harker. Then almost off-handedly, 'Are you saying you *did* shout?'

'No. As far as I knew I was alone. What was the use of . . .'

'To your wife? Did you shout down to her?'

'No.'

'Why not?'

'She was dead.' His eyes moistened a little, but not enough to bring tears. 'You know when a person's dead.'

'Long-distance diagnosis?' Harker's tone was sardonic. Without mercy.

'Dammit, sergeant, you *know*.'

'*You* knew.' The come-back was instantaneous. Then a pause and, in a quieter voice, 'You certainly knew.'

Pinter listened, moving his head as each speaker added to the conversation. But it was no longer a conversation. It was moving towards a genuine *interrogation*. He was reminded of a machine he'd once seen. A machine for measuring the tensile strength of metal. A strip of the metal was clamped at each end between jaws. Then the machine was switched on. Slowly – so slowly as to be less than the eye could see – the jaws drew apart. The dial registered the mounting strain. Then, suddenly, the metal stretched, narrowed into a waist and snapped. In a moment. In less than a second, and with a crack that made you blink at its unexpectedness. One moment nothing. The next moment good metal – good steel, perhaps – pulled apart like dough. The pulling-strength that metal had been able to withstand. The power. The impossible-to-imagine strain imposed upon the structure of that metal.

It was there in that room. The needle on the dial had started to move from zero. The metal still held, but it couldn't hold forever.

Duxbury stood up from his chair. Suddenly. Unbending and standing upright as if propelled by a sudden shock.

'Whisky,' he said. 'I could do with a whisky. Who'll join me? Chris?'

'No, thank you.'

'Sergeant?'

Harker shook his head.

'Constable Pinter?'

'No thank you, sir.'

'Harry, you'll have one, won't you?'

'Yes, please.' Harry Duxbury moistened drying lips. 'A double, watered down a little.'

'Thank God. I thought I was going to have to drink alone. That would have been . . .'

'While you're up, bring the diary,' interrupted Harker.

'The – er – the what?'

'The diary.' Harker's hand went to the inside pocket of his jacket.

'We have a search warrant,' said Tallboy sadly.

'We can look for it.' Harker unfolded the foolscap document and held it loosely in his hand. 'In every drawer. In every cupboard. Under every floorboard, if necessary.' He moved the warrant gently, as if to draw Duxbury's attention to it. 'It would be much easier – much less messy – if you just brought it to us.'

'I – I'm being treated like a criminal.' Duxbury's voice was hoarse, but not outraged. 'Like a criminal,' he repeated. Nobody answered him, and he asked, 'Am I allowed to know why?'

'Just bring the diary,' said Harker.

'It's very – it's very personal,' stammered Duxbury.

'Just bring it.'

'Personal thoughts. Things like that. It's not just an ordinary . . .'

'We're not going to publish it.'

'Still . . .' Duxbury swallowed. 'It wasn't meant to be read until . . .'

'*I'm* going to read it.'

'John.' Tallboy's tone had a pleading quality. 'Just bring the diary. You're going to *have* to. You've no choice. Just bring it.'

'There's four volumes,' muttered Duxbury. 'Five, really. I'm into the fifth now. I was writing it, when . . .'

'Just bring the one for now,' said Harker. 'If it covers the last two months – thereabouts – we'll make do with that for the moment.'

'I *haven't* a choice?' He looked at Tallboy.

'No.'

Duxbury shook his head, then walked slowly from the room.

Harry Duxbury rasped, 'What the hell *is* this?'

'We're going to read your father's diary,' said Harker.

'How did *you* know . . .'

'Tricks of the trade.' Harker's smile was tight-lipped. 'We learn he has a diary, we want to read it, that simple.'

'What do you expect to gain?'

'We don't know . . . until we've read it.'

'There's more to this . . .' Harry Duxbury reached forward, took a cigarette from a box and lit it. He coughed a couple of times. 'There's more to this than "inconsistencies".'

'Major inconsistencies,' said Tallboy gently.

'In what way?'

Tallboy sought words in which to wrap his answer, but before he could speak Harker replied.

'If I'm right, if the Fosters are right – and I think they are – your father's a murderer.'

* * *

203

The word was out. It had been spoken. 'Murderer'. Pinter caught his breath as Harker mouthed the word. He glanced at Harry Duxbury and saw the suddenly distended nostrils, the quiver of the jaw muscles and the pallor of his face. He saw the frown of distaste which clouded Tallboy's face. This man Harker was no puller of punches. Rank or riches meant damn-all to him.

Harry Duxbury sucked in deep breaths. Like a man about to walk onto a stage, and trying to counter stage-fright. And yet (and this amazed Pinter) there was no outraged denial. No anger. No outburst of indignation.

Tallboy, too, noticed this, and the frown turned to one of non-understanding. Of puzzlement. He looked at Harker, and saw a man unmoved by what he'd just said. A calm, determined man who seemed to have *expected* this non-response from the son of the man he'd just indirectly accused of the biggest crime in the book.

Nobody spoke. They just waited. Harry Duxbury drawing deeply on the cigarette. Harker drumming his fingers lightly on the curve of his walking stick. Tallboy and Pinter silently wondering what new rabbit might yet be pulled from the hat.

Duxbury returned to the room. In one hand he carried the drink for his son. In the right hand he carried an opened book. He held an empty tumbler to the open pages with a thumb and had an unopened bottle of Black and White whisky tucked under his arm. He handed the drink to Harry Duxbury, then placed the bottle of whisky alongside his chair before holding the book out to Harker.

'Harry arrived before I'd finished the last entry.' He retained the tumbler and turned to walk back to his chair. As he sat down, he reached for the bottle of whisky. 'Today's entry. You can't be more up to date than that.'

It was a quarto-sized, hard-backed book. Bound in red cloth, with narrow feint rules and no margin. Not a cheap book. It was a diary because he'd *made* it into a diary. The days and dates were in underlined block capitals, and the entries were made in easily-readable writing. The writing of a man well-used to handling a pen.

Harker fingered the pages back until he reached the entry for Sunday, October 31st, then began reading.

Duxbury opened the Black and White, poured half a tumbler of neat whisky and took a good gulp. The silence continued, until Harker looked up from the diary.

'Photography,' he said quizzically.

Duxbury looked perplexed.

'I'd like to see some of your photographs,' amplified Harker.

'What photographs?'

'Those you take.'

'I'm sorry. I don't take photographs.' A wan smile. 'I don't even own a decent camera.'

'The café manager . . .'

'Oh, *him*.' Duxbury moved the tumbler in a gentle dismissive gesture. 'It's his hobby. He likes talking about it. I let him. I listen . . . that's all. It can be interesting sometimes.'

'Back-lighting. Focus. Exposure,' murmured Harker.

'*He* knows all about those things.'

'You don't?'

'Only little bits I've picked up from him.'

'He thinks you're an expert.'

'Oh, I doubt that.'

'He *says* you're an expert,' insisted Harker.

'Oh, no.'

'Portraiture,' pressed Harker.

'What?' Duxbury drank more whisky.

'You concentrate on portraiture. He sticks to landscapes. That's what he tells me.'

'He's been pulling your leg, sergeant. I don't know the first . . .'

'There's one way of making sure.' Harker turned to Pinter. 'The whole house, constable. Every drawer. Every cupboard. If it's locked, force it. Collect all the photographs you find, and . . .'

'No!' Duxbury's smile was one of gentle defeat. 'Don't force anything, Constable Pinter.' He fumbled in a trouser pocket for a key-wallet, then selected a key. 'Bottom, right-hand drawer of my desk. In the study. That's where the "photographs" are. Don't break good furniture.'

As Pinter stood up and took the key-wallet, Harker said, 'And the camera.'

'*I* didn't take the photographs, sergeant. I wouldn't know how.'

205

'That's not what I've been told.'

'I don't give a damn what *you've* been told.' The sudden spat of anger sizzled and disappeared, like a water droplet on a hotplate. The smile returned. Apologetic, this time. 'I'm sorry. You're doing your job.' Then sombrely, 'You'll see what *I* was talking about. *I* couldn't take those photographs.'

Harker nodded at Pinter, and Pinter left the room. Harker returned his attention to the diary. Harry Duxbury screwed out what was left of his cigarette into a nearby ash-tray. Tallboy's expression remained deadpan. Nobody spoke until Pinter returned. It was Harker's show.

They were posed photographs, mounted between thin transparent plastic, in a fancy album. The beef-and-brawn boys, shiny with oil and in postures which exaggerated various body muscles. They'd been cut, carefully, from magazines. Some colour. Some black-and-white. Most of the models wore tiny jock-straps. Three were naked.

Harker flipped through the pages, then dropped the album onto the carpet, alongside his chair.

'Satisfied?' asked Duxbury.

'Portraiture . . . of a sort,' observed Harker drily.

Harry Duxbury gasped, 'For God's sake, dad! Why . . .'

'It's not criminal.' Duxbury lifted the tumbler to his lips again. 'They're published for people to look at.'

He took pipe and pouch from his pocket. Packed the bowl of the pipe, then struck a match and blew pungent smoke into the atmosphere of the room. With the pipe in one hand and the tumbler in the other, he leaned back in his chair exuding a gentle air of defiance.

Harker continued to read the diary. At one point his lips moved into a sneering smile, but he read on.

Then he looked up, and said, 'That poison pen letter business. It seems to have upset you.'

'Wouldn't it have upset you?'

'That's why they're sent,' observed Harker.

'What?'

'To upset people.' Harker slipped the postcard from his pocket. 'Why not tell the police?' he asked innocently.

'That's what he wanted.'

'Evans?'

'That's why he sent the damn thing. Court case. Bad publicity.'

'You didn't keep the letter.'

'No. Why should I?'

'Odd.' Harker tapped the edge of the postcard on the opened page of the diary. 'The private detective follows you. You call in at the local nick, tell your tale of woe to the duty sergeant. *He* gets the gist of the letter from the gumshoe. You're a great pal of the chief superintendent, here. But you don't even mention the letter to *him*. Not even off the record.'

'What could Chris have done?'

'What the duty sergeant did. Scare the hell out of Evans. No need for a court case.'

'Wisdom, after the event.' There was a contemptuous quality in the remark.

'Or something else.' Harker held out the postcard. 'That's from Evans. His handwriting?'

Duxbury nodded.

'If you can *call* it handwriting.'

'He wasn't very literate.'

'He could spell. You make that point yourself in the diary. But the handwriting. Remember when we were kids? When we first learned to write? Graph paper, remember? Each letter filled a square. We didn't write. We *drew*.' He glanced at the message on the postcard. 'Like this. Some people "draw" all their lives. Each letter carefully formed. No style. No speed. Nothing.' He stared at the postcard for a moment. 'The easiest thing in the world to copy. To forge. I could do it. Anybody could. *You* could.'

'What's that supposed to mean?'

'Well now . . .' He dropped the postcard onto the photograph album. 'Let's start with a proposition. No more than that . . . just a proposition. That you wrote the poison pen letter, then sent . . .'

'Why the devil should I do . . .'

'. . . it to your wife. She gets this private investigator on your back, and you trot him into the nearest nick. So far, so good. You go home. Big confrontation scheme. Your wife's very much in the wrong, and you can give her as much stick as the fancy takes

207

you . . . again the diary admits that you went a bit overboard.' They all waited as he paused. 'But don't go *too* far. Don't let anybody else see the letter. Don't have a confrontation bust-up with Evans. Things might go wrong. *You* might be in the schnook. So, destroy the letter, and keep the image of outraged innocence intact.'

'Why?' Duxbury swallowed a mouthful of whisky. He held the pipe in his mouth, while he poured more whisky into the tumbler. He returned the bottle to its place alongside his chair and removed the pipe from his mouth. 'Why the devil should I do a thing like that?'

'People do funny things,' said Harker gently. 'Like collecting pictures of muscle-boys.'

Harker was winning. Slowly – like the jaws of the machine testing a metal's tensile strength – he was putting strain on Duxbury . . . and if the strain continued, Duxbury would break. Pinter could feel it, like a silent scream of anguish. Like the metal he'd once watched.

Tallboy, too. He was far too much of a copper not to see the signs. The liquid courage of the whisky. The inability to come out with a straightforward denial. Instead, the counter-question. The old 'Why should I?' part-admission. Harker was carefully building bricks. Brick with straw he hadn't possessed. But Duxbury was providing straw in plenty. The straw of his own reaction. The straw of his own guilt. Oh yes, there was an abundance of straw, from the diary of Duxbury himself. And (credit where due) Harker was an expert brick-maker.

Harry Duxbury held himself rigid. This balding father of his. This man he thought he knew so well. What *was* he? The word murderer had already been used. A terrible word. A terrifying word. A word not used of ordinary people. Of decent people. Of . . . Dear God, he wasn't a fool. This father of his wasn't a fool. He must *know*. This inquisition – this delving into secret recesses – was no matter of clearing up loose ends of an inquest. Had damn-all to do with an *accident*. Therefore, why not fight back? Why not throw the lie back in their teeth? Why just sit there, smoking a pipe and swilling neat whisky, while this Harker person committed *his* sort of 'murder'?

*   *   *

208

'This diary.' Harker looked up and smiled across the hearth at his adversary. Not a smile of friendship. Not even mock-friendship. The smile of a dentist giving assurance that there'll be no pain, when he knows damn well there will. 'It's not *really* a diary, is it? More of a testament addressed to your son. Wouldn't you say?'

'It's a diary,' said Duxbury flatly.

'That too,' agreed Harker.

'You've read it – are reading it – it's a *diary*.'

'An excuse,' said Harker softly. 'An explanation, supposedly from one generation to the next.'

'Supposedly?' Duxbury removed the pipe from his mouth and tasted whisky. 'That's your *forte*, isn't it, sergeant? *Supposing* things?'

'I have an imagination,' smiled Harker. 'I examine things from all angles. I reach conclusions.'

'Skeletons from cupboards,' mocked Duxbury.

'Skeletons don't belong in cupboards. They belong in graveyards.' He chuckled, as if at a private joke. 'Grave-diggers. That's us. We unearth skeletons . . . maggots and all. You pay us. Tax-payers. Rate-payers. *You* pay us, but you can't stop us. The immaculate Frankenstein monster. You create us, but you can't control us.'

'The monster was a pathetic creature.'

'Ah, but it couldn't be destroyed.'

'For God's sake!' breathed Harry Duxbury.

'Your son's anxious. Worried, perhaps. Possibly even frightened. The son you "talk" to in this diary.'

'And is that wrong?'

'To be admired,' admitted Harker. 'If it was *only* your son.'

'Your imagination again.'

'Oh, no. Your wife, too. Anybody who cared to look. It wasn't kept locked away. It was there to read. Addressed to your son, but *meant* for your wife.'

'Why the devil should I . . .'

'It's on every page. Every entry.' Harker's words were like lashes from a whip. 'Read between the lines. Recognise what you're *really* saying. 'She was a shrew . . . but I loved her. Impossible to live with, an embarrassment, a cruel, selfish

209

bitch . . . but I loved her. Aren't I good? Aren't I a saint? Have you ever met anybody as long-suffering as I am?" That's what you're saying, Duxbury. That's what you're hammering home.'

'She's dead,' said Duxbury softly.

'Of course she's dead. She was impossible to live with.'

Harry Duxbury caught his breath. Both Tallboy and Pinter leaned fractionally forward. Not *quite* the complete accusation. But so near. So bloody *near*! An innocent man's reaction? Outrage? Anger? Shock?

Duxbury took his pipe from his mouth, gulped whisky and remained silent. Harker gave him time. Enough time – more than enough time – to digest the last remark. To construe its meaning. To say *something*, but Duxbury clamped the pipe stem between his teeth and said nothing.

'She read it.' Harker's voice softened slightly. 'She read it, because she was *expected* to read it.'

'It's possible.' The tone was lifeless. Expressionless.

'A way of getting your own back. Of repaying her for making *your* life hell.'

'She's dead.' He repeated the two words he'd spoken before, as if they explained and excused everything.

'She's dead,' echoed Harker. 'Let's concentrate on the day she died. Why take that walk along the cliffs?'

'We were holidaying. Why not?'

'I know that path. In summer it's safe enough. In winter, after rain, it's muddy. Filthy. Slippery.'

'We didn't know that.'

'You weren't fresh-air enthusiasts. Neither of you.'

'No.' Again the tumbler was raised to his lips.

'The diary again.' Harker touched the open pages. 'You'd had a fight that night.'

'It wasn't *so* unusual.'

'But next morning you strolled together. Like two lovers.'

'You've read the diary . . . not *quite* like lovers.'

'But together.'

'Yes.'

'The last walk of her life.'

'So it turned out.'

'Why?' asked Harker softly.

'What?'

'*Why* was it the last walk of her life?'

'That's an idiotic question, sergeant.'

'Fine . . . give me an equally idiotic answer.'

'She slipped. She fell from the cliff. She killed herself.'

'And you didn't try to save her? Catch her as she fell?'

'There wasn't time.'

'But time to stand looking down at her?'

'I was shocked.'

'Shocked? Or making sure?'

'I don't understand.'

'That she was out of her misery?'

'Riddles.' He shook his whisky-befuddled head. 'Now we're talking in riddles.'

'I quote.' Harker read from the diary. ' "She was free . . . The end of her unhappy life . . . In the last few years her life must have been hell".' He looked up. 'In short, she was out of her misery. *What* misery?'

'I – I don't remember . . .'

'A record of your thoughts, as you looked down at her.'

'I was still in a state of shock. She'd just . . .'

'Not when the diary entry was made. You were here. Back home. The inquest was over. Shock, perhaps. *Some* shock. But you knew what you were writing. So . . . *what* misery?'

'I don't know. How the hell do I know?' He emptied the tumbler, placed the cold pipe on a stand ash-tray, then slopped more whisky into the glass. 'You tell *me*. You're the oracle. You know all the answers. You tell me . . . tell us *all*.'

'I think I could,' said Harker softly.

'Go ahead then. Be my guest.' He waved the tumbler. 'Say what you have to say. You have an audience. Make the most of it.'

'Thirty years ago. Maybe a little more, maybe a little less, but we'll settle for thirty. Thereabouts.' He started slowly. Carefully. As if telling a well-loved fairy story to a small group of eager youngsters. And they all listened. Even Duxbury tried to focus his mind to listen to the words, and make sense of them. 'A young couple in love. Very much in love. He was ambitious. Had the future all planned, and knew he could do it. She was an only child. A bit rebellious. Knew her own mind. Spoke that mind. Of the two, she was the dominating character. Not too bad, of course. Not in those days. And he couldn't see it, because they were very much in love.

'A nice couple. Innocent. They liked each other's company. No more than that. No messing around. No "trial runs". The sort of love you find in romantic novels. In Hilton's *Goodbye Mister Chips*. Cycling through the Yorkshire Dales. Listening to jazz records. Maybe going to the cinema. Holding hands. Kissing, perhaps. I think kissing, but no more than kissing. They were in love. Make no mistake about it, they *were* in love. Completely. And very innocently.'

Duxbury rested both forearms along the arms of the chair. The tumbler was tipped a little. His head was bowed, with his chin resting on his chest and, despite the input of booze (or, perhaps, *because* of it) his gaze seemed to be concentrated on a point a long distance away . . . or a long time ago.

'They married,' continued Harker. 'They married in the teeth of opposition from her parents. Who knows? Perhaps her parents knew. Or guessed. Perhaps her father. But we're not talking about today. We're not talking about a time when anything and everything can be discussed. Not the swinging society. Not the bed-hopping crowd. We're talking about a time – not too long ago – and a stratum of society when certain subjects were taboo. When they *couldn't* be talked about. So, all her parents could do was object. Object on silly, unimportant grounds. And it meant nothing. They were in love, so they married.

'That honeymoon. It doesn't matter where it was. Or how long it was. They were both virgins.' He paused. A beautifully timed pause then, almost sadly, 'I never married. I can't talk from experience. I can only tell you what I've been told. That when neither party has had experience, a honeymoon can be something of a disaster. A heartbreaking farce. It can happen with normal people. It can be a time of total embarrassment. Almost shame. But they get over it. They can even laugh at it later.

'But these two – these two young people – *they* couldn't laugh at

212

it. Ever! They made a discovery. That he was impotent. Totally, absolutely impotent. And it wasn't a temporary thing. Oh yes, I'm told that happens sometimes. The newly married status. The first woman a man beds being the one woman he loves. It can bring about a temporary impotence. Maybe they thought that was it . . . at first. But it wasn't. It was permanent. *Forever*. The physical side of marriage wasn't theirs to enjoy. Never would be. And when *that* realisation sank home things changed.'

Tallboy knew he was witnessing something not too far removed from magic. This story. It was hitting gold time and time again. But from what? Inspired guesswork? A form of policing even *he* had never seen before? God knew, only that there was enough truth to hammer at what defences Duxbury still had like a power-driven battering-ram. The man at the receiving end – the man who'd dared Harker to tell the story – was breathing like somebody dragged from the sea. Long, harsh breaths, as if his lungs were incapable of holding enough air without conscious, physical effort.

And still Harker continued.

'There was a child. A son. Obviously not *his* son. An affair, perhaps. Maybe even a contrived affair. Some women *need* children. Feel incomplete without them. It's a reason for getting married. One of the reasons. Whatever, she gave birth to a son. And the man accepted the child as *his* son. It was, if you like, proof to the world that he was capable of fathering a son. It buried his secret. It was his "proof" to the rest of the world, even though, physically, the son bore no resemblance to either of his parents.

'There were no half-measures. The man accepted the son without qualification. He loved his son. Gave him everything a man could ever give to his son. He even put it into words. Written words. "I have a good son. A fine son. A very wise son." Those words were not empty. They came from the heart, and were directed to the one person the man truly loved.'

Harker paused. It was a long pause, as if he were marshalling his thoughts for the next stage of his story. That, or there were details he couldn't fill in. Didn't want to guess at. A long pause with three of his listeners silent and waiting.

At last he said, 'Marriages go wrong. Lots of marriages. Sometimes for trivial reasons. Sometimes for more important reasons. They go wrong, and usually it's a very gradual process. And whatever we may think in our middle and elder years, impotence in the prime of life is not a trivial reason. A marriage never consumated. Never consumated, but because she married against the express wishes of her parents, the wife had to keep *that* to herself. Her pride forced her to keep it a secret. In effect, she'd married a eunuch.

'A charade, then. A charade of normality. Of respectability. A husband, but *not* a husband. A son, but *not* the son of the man the world took to be his father. The strain was more than she could take. Whatever she'd once been, she gradually became embittered. Sour. Her personality changed. The son married, and she hated his wife. She couldn't *help* herself. This younger woman – this comparative stranger – was *truly* married. Happily married. *Completely* married. In honesty, I think the woman's feelings – her hurt – were something well beyond the comprehension of any man.'

Harry Duxbury breathed, 'That means . . .' but Tallboy put out a hand, touched his arm, and silenced him.

Duxbury was crying. Motionless, still staring into space, but the tears were running down his cheeks, unheeded. He was broken. Smashed, beyond repair. But Harker wasn't yet finished.

'The man,' continued Harker. 'The husband. The other half of this life-long make-believe. He, too, had his burden. A heavy one, and one he daren't share, even with his wife. Least of all with his wife. I've already said . . . we're discussing a level of society where "respectability" is everything. An old fashioned society, still clinging to Victorian principles of morality. He's impotent. But gradually he discovers he's also something else. Something, in his eyes, even worse.

'He's a homosexual. God knows what he felt when *that* realisation dawned. His shame. His self-contempt. The knowledge that with another man he might *not* be impotent. Because he still loved his wife. That I don't doubt for a minute. In his own fashion – in his own non-carnal way – he still loved her. That being the case, his own honesty – his own sense of humour – prevented him from ever taking the body of a man in preference to *her* body. To be safe, to deny himself even the temptation, he refused to join

214

the all-male organisations of which he could have been a part. A Masonic Lodge, perhaps. The Round Table crowd. Anything along those lines was out. What he was – what he recognised himself to be – frightened him. Terrified him. Who knows? Maybe a more terrible secret than the first. Certainly more personal.

'Think about it. A man who believed himself to be unnatural. Foul. Bestial. That's the belief he had to live with. He even pandered to that belief . . . just a little and in secret. Photographs of men. Beautiful men. Desirable men. He cut them from magazines and kept them in an album, locked away in his desk. To look at, you understand. Nothing more. In effect, they were *his* pin-ups . . . and as unattainable as the normal man's pictures of female models.'

Pinter wished it would stop. Almost prayed for it to stop. This stripping to the soul of a man he'd previously respected. Nobody had the right to do to another human being what Harker was doing to Duxbury. Nobody had the right to play God, like this. Nobody!

Tallboy, too, wondered when it would end. Not *where* it would end. It would end with the complete crack-up of Duxbury. Nothing surer. The man was already like a crumbling structure, and Harker was placing the demolition charges in place. When he pressed the plunger . . .

He (Tallboy) had played the interview game scores of times. Hundreds of times. But never like this. Never as devastatingly as *this*. Indeed, it wasn't an interview, in the real sense. No questions. No seeking, no probing. Just a 'story' told quietly and without emotion. But it was far, far more effective than any questioning. Far more destructive. Far more cruel.

'The marriage,' continued Harker gently. 'What marriage can withstand that sort of strain? The mental strain? A little like putting the man's mind – and the woman's mind – through a shredding machine. It *had* to produce a form of madness. A souring of what had once been genuine affection.

'The woman went first. Her bitterness grew. Contempt. Disgust. If not hatred, a particular form of loathing. In her eyes, a husband who wasn't even a *man*. She thought nothing of humiliating him. I don't even think she *knew* she was humiliating him. It became her way of life. Her way of living. And, for a long

215

time, the husband accepted it. A form of penance, perhaps. He withdrew into himself. At home he spent hours alone in his study. Brooding. Heartbroken, maybe, but unable to see a way out of things. She retreated into the Never-Never-Land of cheap romantic novels. Neither tried to understand the other, because neither *could* understand the other. There was no point of contact. That first love – those trips into the Dales – this is what it had grown into.'

Harker moved his walking stick. It had been alongside him, and he shifted it to a position between his knees. The rubber ferrel was just in front of his shoes, and he rested his hands on the crook. The impression was that of a pulpit. An attitude of deliberate denunciation. But if so, a sad denunciation. There was no joy in his tone. No satisfaction. A thankless job had to be done, and luck had thrown him into the position where *he* had to do it. Bad luck. But it *had* to be done.

'We come to the diary,' he sighed. 'In this story – this story you asked me to tell – the man kept a diary. A good diary in which he, at first, recorded an occasional thought. The diary wasn't locked away. Why should it be? It was, if anything, a record of his life, to be read – perhaps with interest, perhaps with nostalgia – by his son after the man's death. He knew his wife read the diary. How did he know? That's not important. Perhaps he popped it into its drawer one night and he found it on the desk next time he saw it. It isn't important. Just that *she* read it. That wasn't important either. Not at first. The record of a good man. Nothing to be ashamed of. Nothing she shouldn't see. A hint of his torment, perhaps. Maybe more than a hint. What matter? The only torment mentioned was that which they shared. Maybe a means of letting her know things. Of saying things he daren't say to her face, and in circumstances in which she couldn't answer back.

'That at first. But gradually – not too long ago – he realised something. The diary could be a weapon. Oh yes, things had got that far. Weapons! He'd been hurt too often. Suffered too much. He wanted her to suffer, too. So he used the diary. Entries calculated to hurt. Entries he knew she'd read.' He paused, then very carefully continued, 'There's an entry about a poison-pen letter, accusing him of having an affair. A letter *he* sent. Why?

216

Simple. To make her believe he was only impotent as far as *she* was concerned. That *she* carried the guilt. That he was what he was – how he was – only with *her*.

'There's another entry. Before the poison-pen letter entry. About a business trip. The Saffron Hotel. A very detailed entry. A woman. Not a pick-up. Not some cheap tart. A decent, comparatively well-off widow of about his own age. Like him she was staying at the hotel that night. On her way to the south coast. They were drawn to each other. They went to bed together. The entry gives details, but without in any way being salacious.'

Harker looked across at Duxbury and said, 'I could end my story at this point, Duxbury. I know the rest. It has to be told. Either you or I. In fairness, I give you the choice.'

Duxbury raised his head. His crumpled face and tear-stained cheeks mirrored the emotion tearing him apart. He sniffed, emptied the tumbler, then placed it on the carpet.

'Fairness?' he croaked.

'You have no more secrets,' said Harker gently. 'None.'

'Who are you? *What* are you?' groaned Duxbury.

'A detective,' said Harker simply. 'I check things. Everything! I learn about people. I reach conclusions . . . the only conclusions fitting the facts. Fitting all the things I've checked.'

'Tell it.' Duxbury closed his eyes for a moment. 'Tell it. You've got it all right so far. Tell the rest.'

He rested his elbows on his knees, leaned forward and covered his face with his hands.

Harker rested his hands on the walking-stick-pulpit for a moment, then continued.

'That entry. That Saffron Hotel entry. It was a lie. A well-told, beautifully-constructed lie. I know. I breakfasted at the Saffron this morning. Harry Duxbury told me about the visit. A piece of thistledown, but it had to be checked. To check that he *had* been at that hotel. A fine hotel. A good breakfast. I asked questions, and they were answered. I was shown the register. He'd booked in. Stayed the night. On that date, nobody else stayed overnight. No woman. Nobody! Nobody had stayed overnight for three days before. Nor until a week afterwards. A "seasonal" hotel. Just John Duxbury within a period of ten days. Check and double-check with

217

the staff. Only John Duxbury. The woman in the entry doesn't exist. Never existed.

'But the entry in the diary was for a purpose. It served its purpose, and it was followed by the mock poison-pen letter. That was the state of affairs, the state of the Duxbury marriage, when John and Maude Duxbury went on that last weekend together. What happened on that last weekend? What degree of hurt and humiliation they inflicted upon each other on their last night together? I don't know. Only one person *does* know. What I *do* know is that it led to murder.

'A little reconstruction, perhaps. That walk on the cliff tops. They thought they were alone. That tricky stretch of the path, and a fall to almost certain death. Let's say a temptation that wasn't resisted. Just one push . . . then perhaps regrets. Oh yes, I think you regretted it, Duxbury. Before she reached the foot of the cliff. But it was too late. That's why you stood there. Watching. Hoping she *wasn't* dead. Possibly considering the question of jumping off yourself. Making it a double-header. Too late, of course. Like so many people who kill. Sorry . . . a split second too late.

'Things went their own course. The inquest. The verdict. Without even trying, you'd committed the perfect murder. But you'd been seen. Foster had seen everything through his binoculars. A timid man. A foolish man. But, eventually, he reported what he'd seen. That's why *I'm* here, Duxbury. That's why I've talked all this time. Talked long enough. Now it's your turn.'

'Dad.' Harry Duxbury stood up, then knelt alongside the older man and put an arm across his shoulder. He breathed, 'Dad. Tell this lying hound he's wrong. Throw the lie back in his teeth. Tell him he's . . .'

'No!' Duxbury raised his head, he looked at the man he knew as 'son', and his face was ugly with hurt, but his voice, though soft, was steady. 'He's *right*. Everything! The marriage. The Saffron Walden Hotel. The letter. Even that damn diary. There isn't a flaw in what he's said.'

'You – you . . .'

'I pushed her.' The three-word confession rode on a deep sigh. 'Before she even toppled, I was sorry. But it was too late.'

218

The younger man buried his face in John Duxbury's shoulder, and his whole frame shook with his sobbing.

The soft tick of a clock could be heard in the silence. From beyond the walls of the house a screech owl called. Then Tallboy spoke.

'Do the rest, sergeant,' he muttered.

Harker hoisted himself stiffly to his feet, then shook his head.

'That's why you're here,' he said flatly.

'What?' Tallboy looked almost frightened.

'I've done my job.' Harker closed the diary and dropped it onto the seat he'd just vacated. 'Anything else . . . that's up to you. Or, if you haven't the stomach, Constable Pinter will obey orders.'

'Dammit, you can't . . .'

'I *can*.' Harker stared into the face of the chief superintendent for a moment, then said, 'Don't try calling Foster as a witness. He won't play. Don't try calling *me*. I'll tell you to go to hell . . . in as many words. All those pips and crowns. All the yes-sir-no-sir-three-bags-full-sir you're fed every day of your life. They're supposed to mean you can make decisions. Go ahead. Make one. You know the truth. Live with it. Try proving it. *Shove* it, as far as I'm concerned. I've had a gutful. There's a detective chief inspector I have to report to. He's a wishy-washy bastard, too. He'll believe whatever I tell him . . . unless you tell him something else, first.'

Harker turned and hobbled from the room.

PART FOURTEEN

The End of the Cul-De-Sac

'I do not,' snapped Briggs, 'enjoy having my balls chewed off by strange chief superintendents. And where the hell have *you* been since you left Duxbury's place?'

'In bed,' yawned Harker. 'I'm going back there when you've finished giving your tonsils an airing.'

Briggs was slinging rank, and not getting very far. It was his way of demonstrating that he was a frightened man, and Harker knew it.

'Bed!' Briggs glared. 'I sent you out to . . .'

'I'll say to you what I said to him,' interrupted Harker wearily. 'Shove it.'

'You said *that* to a . . .'

'I'm a sergeant. I carry the responsibilities of a sergeant. When I reach *your* rank – when I reach *his* rank – I'll carry *that* responsibility. Not,' he added hurriedly, 'that that will ever happen. I have some say in the matter. But, as you remind me, you "sent me out". Now I'm back.'

'You – you don't give a damn, do you?' spluttered Briggs.

'About some things. Important things.'

'Murder, for example?'

'Did Tallboy mention murder?'

'No.' Briggs cooled down a little. 'He said you'd . . .'

'So, why bring the subject up?'

'Harry.' The ersatz-anger gave way to pleading. 'You know what I have to know. Why I sent you off like that. Now, for Christ's sake, *tell me.*'

'Foster's a very honest man,' said Harker flatly.

'So that means . . .'

'But even honest men make mistakes, sometimes.'

'What you're saying is . . .'

'You have a verdict. Coroners don't like coppers twisting their tails. How many verdicts do you want?'

'Look, if Foster pushes the complaint . . .'

'Foster couldn't push a key into a lock.'

'Harry . . . *please!*'

Harker stared at the man behind the desk, and did nothing to hide his contempt. The hell, why *should* he put his neck on the chopping-block for this make-believe detective chief inspector? Let him sit there behind his fancy desk, in his fancy office. Let him *earn* his corn for a change. That or starve. Or suffer.

'Don't ever come the "please Harry" to me again, Briggs,' he growled. 'You sent me out there to find the truth. Okay, I found it, but it stays inside there.' He tapped his forehead gently with a finger. 'You want to be satisfied with the verdict you already have? Fine. I won't complain. You want a recorded murder on the books? Same again. Fine. Just don't make me your conscience any more. Ever! Spin a coin. Cut cards. Read tea leaves. I don't give a damn. Just reach *your* decision.'

'Harry, you can't . . .'

'Sit there and watch.' Harker pushed himself from the chair. 'And the name is Detective Sergeant Harker, *sir.*'

He limped from the office, closing the door quietly behind him.